Guns, Gold and True Love

By
Theodore Potter

PotterHouse Publishing

PotterHouse Publishing LLC
Tok, Alaska 99780

For information, Contact the author, Theodore Potter at potterlwen@hotmail.com

Tags: Western, Novel, Western pioneer, gold prospecting, turn of the century adventure, 1900 adventure

DEDICATION

For Fern, My loving and talented wife.

CHAPTER ONE

The rider was hungry. Not the starving type of hunger, but the, "I could eat the west end of an east bound buffalo type hunger." He hadn't had any food to speak of since that last town down on the Rio Grand river, near the border town of Nogalas. He had been called out by two slicks, that needed a rung up the ladder to fame as gunfighters. He killed the first because he didn't have time to talk any sense into his pea brain. The man was fast, but slow compared to him. The other died simply because he didn't have the gumption to stop himself in time. As usual, Brandon was sicker than an old dog after it was over and after he had defended himself with the local Marshal, went outside and threw up all over the ground. Since the Marshal had suggested he might want to move along, he did just that and had bought no supplies, which had been his mission to that town in the first place.

Now four days and one hundred miles later he was damn sure half starved.

Brandon Chedlow had traveled north for four days, without seeing a single living soul or any food and now was looking over a ridge at a small lake, where he could see multiple animal tracks in the mud, around the edges of the water. As he waited for some game to come to water, so he could shoot it, his mind wandered back to West Virginia where he grew up in the Appalachian Mountains.

Brandon Chance Chedlow was a third generation American. His great grandfather had immigrated to America from the north British Isles, when his grandfather was four years old and followed the printers trade in Baltimore, Maryland. His Grandfather had chosen not to be a printer and moved down to Charleston, West Virginia. He met and married a native mountain lass, that begat him two sons and one daughter. Brandon was a product of the youngest son Darren's marriage, to a loose woman named Luizzy. The only thing Luizzy reckoned she ever did right, was birth him as a son, but that wasn't enough to keep her around and by the time Brandon turned four, she had already found someone else and moved on. What hurt Brandon so, was that she never even said goodbye. He remembered crying for weeks and asking his father where his mother was. One day his father lost it and swiped him up beside the head and made his ears ring. Brandon stopped crying and loving his father on that very day.

He became completely self-reliant on one person and that person was himself. He didn't always get it right in those first years, but he wore his lumps well, learned his lessons and shared not one thing with anyone. His father had always been a drinker and stayed blitzed most of the time on moonshine. When Brandon reached eleven he was a six foot slim boy, that everyone thought of as a man. He discovered books and taught himself to read. Sometime he would read all night if the book was good. At first he skipped over the big words until he began to fit them with the story. By the time he was eleven he never skipped over words, because he had been given a dictionary by someone and he would stop and look up the meaning.

He became interested in guns at the age of thirteen and not having one, he whittled a six gun out of pine. His holster consisted of one piece of leather folded and sewn together and two slits for the belt. He had to remake that holster three times before he got it right. After trying to fast draw the dummy gun, he tied the holster down with a length of rawhide. He would go out in the woods and practice his fast draw.

He was doing that one day, when he saw a man sitting on a horse watching him, from the edge of the forest. The man said, "Can't kill much with that wooden stick can you boy?"

Brandon looked at him and returned with, "I won't always have a stick for a gun mister, someday I'll have a real one."

The man who seemed about thirty, spat chewing tobacco over in the opposite direction and said, "Just what would you shoot with a real gun boy?"

Brandon answered with "Well, nothing that didn't need shooting sir."

The man began to like him after that and said, "Why don't you come over to my place over yonder and sit on the front porch and talk a spell?"

Brandon said, "That sounds fine mister, what did you say your name was sir?"

The man laughed and replied with, "I didn't boy, but it's Charley, come on and I'll give you some good vittles, you look hungry son. He had made a good friend that day and if old Charley hadn't of caught the flu that winter and died he would still be his friend.

A movement caught his eye on the far side of the small lake. He brought his Henry up beside him and cocked it. A horse and colt appeared and drank from the lake. He relaxed and his thoughts turned back to when old Charley had made friends with him.

Charley was the epitome of all Mountain Men, he didn't care for work in the normal sense anyhow and only went to work if he was hungry or thirsty. He would disappear for an hour and return with a big buck across his horse or slap together a working pot of moonshine which he always had making.

He loaned Brandon an old war cap and ball six gun for him to practice with. It took Brandon some hard work to learn to load the thing, but he finally got it right. The first round he pulled off scared the crap out of him and he missed the tin can by four feet. Charley almost peed himself he laughed so hard and caused the only harsh word that would be passed between the two. Brandon said, "Shut up!" Charley passed it off, but never laughed at this too serious kid again. Brandon apologized later and was sorry he had said it.

Brandon heard something coming and saw a big mountain Lion approach with slow stealth. He had heard somewhere that Lions were good to eat, but he was holding out for venison.

He remembered the terrible flu epidemic that took Charley that winter. He hadn't seen Charley for two days. Usually Charley came over and got

Brandon every day and give him a ride to his place on his horse. It was a good six mile walk there and back with a couple of pretty good hills in between. On the third day Brandon packed some lunch and took off on foot. He knew something was wrong before he opened the door. His friend was only barely alive. He was burning up with fever and had no water near him. Brandon ran to the well and pulled a cold fresh bucket of water, spilling some in his haste. Charley was almost out of his head and had fouled his bed clothing. Brandon let him drink as much water as he wanted and then began cleaning his friend up. He almost lost his breakfast a few times, but this was his only friend and he had to do what he had to do. Charley was mumbling something and then he grabbed his friend and clearly said, "My will", and pointed at the kitchen table.

Charley was dying and knew it. Brandon slowly walked to the table and looked at the paper. He turned and Charlie's eyes had followed him. He reached down and picked them up and read the front page and dropped them on the table and ran to Charley and hugged him begging God not to take his only friend, but the death rattle in Charley's throat told it all. Charley took one big breath and when it came out, he died. Brandon was numb with pain and couldn't believe this man had been alive and well just a few days ago. He went out and fed the horse some grain and hay. The water trough needed filling as well, so he did that too. He knew his friend had to be buried quickly and that there was a good chance he would come down with the same killer flu that killed Charley. He had dug two graves side by side and if he began to feel he was getting sick he was going to crawl in the spare one before he died.

A young doe came down to water, but he didn't shoot, although his gut was rumbling like crazy. He would wait for a buck and kill him. He went back to remembering.

He hadn't gotten sick, however his father had succumbed to the evil bug and Brandon had to bury him as well. He decided he didn't want any more contact with any relatives that might come along, so he took the one horse, long gun and pistol with ammo and some clothes and moved to Charley's place that belonged to him now. He took many days to make the move complete.

After some three months of being alone, he boarded up the cabin and lit out west. He was lightning fast on the draw and always hit his target. He had money that Charley had gave him instruction on its where abouts. He had two good horses and a wonder lust that must be sated. He rode west to Saint Louis and joined a whisky boat for a trip to the great falls on the upper Missouri River. The Montana, Territory, was wild and unsettled. He wanted to see it all, but weather had got in the way and he found he had to move south for the winter. The Montana winter was unforgiving in its cold. His native West Virginia was cold in winter, but this cold could kill a man in a few minutes. He traveled south to the Mexican Border and had run into trouble in Nogalas and been told to move on

. Now he was trying to kill his dinner on a lake in central Texas. He couldn't believe his eyes! There on his left was a four point buck sniffing the air and approaching the water. He put his Henry sites on the deer's chest and when the deer brought his head up from drinking pulled the round off and the deer jumped high in the air and died in a heap. Brandon walked to his horse, mounted and quickly rode to his deer before some other predator could lay claim to the kill. The buck weighed no more than a hundred pounds, so he lifted it up and threw it across his saddle and rode to a bunch of trees on the creek that fed this lake. He found a good camp site then gutted and skinned the deer. He saw there was some rocks over the way and began stripping the venison for drying, so it would last and not go rancid on him. He cut some of the back strap out and put it on a spit of green willow over a hot fire and the aroma was making his stomach juices boil and his mouth to water. He couldn't wait and took the spit down and cut some meat from the outside that was golden brown and as soon as it cooled he ate like a starving hound.

CHAPTER TWO

Brandon stayed in that camp for three days until all the deer meat he hadn't eaten was dry. When meat is all someone has to eat, It took a lot of it to satisfy one's hunger. He was thankful he had some salt, it made the meat much more palatable by flavoring it.

On the third day he packed his bed roll and the deer meat and rode west by north. The pan handle of Texas in 1886 was a wild mostly unsettled part of the west. Towns were few and far between and he had to watch out for water because there wasn't much of that out here either. Brandon was twenty-one years old and had a reputation of being a fast gun. It wasn't that he was angry with anyone, but now he had to wear his six shooter or some drunk would shoot him down for the heck of it.

He rode into the town of Odessa, Texas and saw it was no more than a few Mexicans and a hand full of white folks, with an Indian or two thrown in for good measure. There was a trading post and livery. He shopped for food staples: flour, bacon, coffee and sugar to make his coffee a little sweet. There was a bar and he thought he might need to wet his whistle with something cold. He entered the saloon and walked to the bar. A person of indeterminate age and possibly a female, asked in a gruff voice, what in hell he wanted. He looked her in the eye and said, "If your beer is cool, I'll have a glass."

The person returned with, "If you don't think it's cool enough just go on to the next place mister."

This sat Brandon back on his heels a bit and he said, "I'm sorry, I didn't mean to ruffle your feathers mam I'd like a beer just fine, thank you."

There was another man at the bar and things took a turn for the worse when he piped up with, "Kind of young to be drinking ain't you hombre."

At first Brandon took no notice of the man because he knew the type. He was a local that tried to stir up trouble, just because he was bored with life in this piss pot of a town. The man pushed his luck by saying: "I was talking to you, you young whippersnapper."

He faced Brandon as he said it. Brandon looked at the bartender and then shrugged his shoulders. He turned to the gunman and began to talk. He said, "I know you don't want to die this day mister, so let me tell you, that if you draw on me you will. Let me buy you a beer and we'll have a drink together."

Brandon saw the raw emotions take toll on the man and thought he was going to start his draw. Brandon decided he didn't want to throw up the venison he had consumed for breakfast and in a blur pulled his piece and placed the barrel against the man's forehead between his eyes. The man's eyes crossed and he pissed his pants right there. The barmaid looked over the bar and almost laughed out loud. Brandon reached down and took the gun from his would be assailant's holster and placed it on the bar. The bar maid grabbed it and put it somewhere behind the bar. Brandon said, "Now mister why don't you go on home and sleep it off and watch who you draw down on from now on."

The would be gunfighter all but run out of the bar. The barmaid did laugh then and made Brandon smile. The lady said, "My name's Bertha, what's yours fellow?"

Brandon told her and her eyes grew big and she said, "Some fellow came through here a time ago and told us about you and the trouble you had down in Nogalas. He said he had never seen anybody draw that fast before and now I believe him. Here is a beer on the house and welcome to Odessa, Texas."

The little town was too small to hold Brandon for long and he said goodbye to old Bertha, then rode northwest into the Oklahoma, Panhandle. He had some new feelings now that he had spared that man's life back there and thought maybe he might be a candidate for a lawman someday. Who knows, however, which way the winds would blow. He would take each day as it came and not ask for more than his share from life.

For the most part Brandon was happy with his lot in life. He still missed his friend Charley and wished he hadn't died on him. He had a good horse named, of all things, Charley. As far as Brandon knew the horse had no name before he became its owner, but since he had come by the animal via Charley, why not call him by that name. He was impressed by how well the brown horse adapted to the trail, because he remembered Charley saying, that horse was born here and will likely die here. Charley become attached to Brandon as well and would come at his whistle every time.

.

CHAPTER THREE

Horse and rider rode north east out of Odessa, down into the Brazos valley and stopped at waters edge and Brandon slid out of the saddle and went down on his hands and knees to drink from the sweet water. He and Charley had been without water for a full day and were dehydrated to the point it would have been critical from now on.

Brandon and Charley camped on the Brazos where Brandon shot another buck. Plenty of food and the company of a fine horse, made Brandon think what else could a man need. Deep in his heart he knew there was something else he wanted, but he couldn't put his finger on it.

Brandon decided to try and catch some of the rainbow trout that whizzed by his camp all the time in the stream. He had no fishing line so he thought of any other method he might use. He looked at some reeds growing at the water's edge and thought maybe he could make a basket or something and catch fish that way. He cut reeds by the arm load and set them in the hot Texas sun to dry. He had never weaved anything before and had a hard time getting started, but finally he had a basket of sorts going. The thing looked for all the world like an out of shape bushel basket when he finished. He shucked his boots and rolled his pant legs up and waded out till he was up to his knees, then waited for a fish to come by. He didn't have to wait long because he was an attraction to them and they swam circles around his bare legs. He tried dipping a fish, but the basket was too tight and only held water. Then he decided to simply set the basket down on some fish. He trapped some and could feel them running into the basket attempting to escape. He looked down at the closed bottom of the basket and he got it. He took his Barlow pocket knife out of his pants pocket and cut most of the bottom out. He looked down at four good sized rainbows swimming around in the basket. He reached down and picked one up and flipped it on the bank. He picked up the basket and allowed the others to go about their business. He could only eat one fish at a setting and hadn't the room to carry dried fish with him now. He was extremely proud of his fishing trap and he folded it away for future use.

CHAPTER FOUR

Brandon rode leisurely north along the New Mexico territory border while staying over in Texas. He eventually came to the small town of Dalhart, Texas, where the trail turned west towards Salano, New Mexico. Dalhart was a wild cattle town where wild cowboys were getting drunk after a drive of hundreds of miles of ranging cows from south Texas on the way to Denver and the stockyards there. The herds were bedded down outside of town and half of the crew turned loose with half pay on the town. The two saloons and one whore house was open all night and day. Brandon did his best to dodge trouble, but he needed a few things in this town. For one thing Old Charley was about to go lame from a loose shoe and he wanted to get all four shoes replaced anyhow. He found the livery and there was a blacksmith beside it. He made a deal for the blacksmith to shoe his horse and take him to the livery for the night, then he went looking for a room to sleep in and a real bath with soap and hot steamy water.

The one hotel was a shoddy affair quickly thrown up long ago and made Brandon almost change his mind about sleeping there, but once inside it wasn't all that bad. If things began falling down around his ears, he would bail out the window. The barber shop held the only bath house in town and he felt pretty good with clean clothes on and a clean body to match. He found a steak house and ordered a Huge "T" bone with all the trimmings. He thought when the waitress brought the thing that maybe he had messed up and ordered two, but it was only one. He tore into it and was surprised at the tenderness of the meat. The baked potato was something he had never experienced before. He did figure the butter was for that tuber and smeared it lavishly on the potatoes. He found it delicious and ate skin and all. He ran out of room and had to quit eating. He thought about sitting there until he was hungry again, but that would take hours and he wanted to see some ladies anyhow, so he paid up and went to one of the two saloons in town.

There was a crowd at the bar and almost every table was full. He found space at the bar and bellied up. The bartender looked like a throwback to Neanderthal intelligence, but when he spoke he was every bit as nice as old Charley had been and Brandon liked him. He ordered a beer and after paying, took it to one of the empty tables and sat down. A bar girl was there in an instant and asked if she could set with him. He indicated she was welcome and volunteered to buy her a drink. She was younger than he was and painted to high heaven with garish looking paint or something. She took the drink and downed it in one gulp. It looked like whisky, but on the way back to the bar he tasted it and it was sassafras tea. He told the bartender he needed a bottle of the best whisky in the house and to give the lady another drink too. He paid for them and returned to the table. The girl downed the shot of sassafras and before she could stop him he uncapped the bottle and poured her a shot of whisky in her shot glass. The girl looked at the bartender who shrugged his shoulders and held both hands out as if to say, what do you want me to do about it girl. The girl turned to Brandon and said, "You knew my drink was tea didn't you mister?"

Brandon smiled and nodded his head. She smiled back and said, "If I drink that, I'll want another and then I'll want another until you will have to carry me out of here."

Brandon simply held a hand out palm up and said, "Be my guest."

The girl, with no more hesitation, threw the drink back and Brandon filled her glass once more. Brandon saw the bartender motion to someone at the back of the bar and he knew he had avoided trouble as long as possible. He hadn't taken a drink of whisky and only a few sips of his beer. He saw a big fellow coming towards them pretending he wasn't. Brandon loosened his six shooter and prepared himself for some kind of fight. What happened was far beyond what he expected. The burly man arrived at their table and reached down and grabbed both arms of the girl and was in the process of lifting her to her feet when she let go a scream of protest and caused Brandon to stand and put his left hand on the man and say, "No friend, leave her alone!"

The bouncer dropped the girl and squared away on his new target. His gun was slung low and he looked like he could use it. Brandon said, "Are you sure you want to do this fellow?"

The man growled and went for his gun. Brandon out drew him in a blur and shot him dead. There was instant silence as Brandon looked the crowd over. There were no other guns being drawn and everyone had seen the town bully beaten to the draw. The girl sat there in shock saying, "O my god you killed Billy, he is the fastest gun around here."

Brandon took his bottle and said, "Are you coming or are you staying here, gal?"

The girl looked at him and over at the now seething bartender and jumped up and said, "What do you think buster?"

Brandon laughed at that. The two walked out and over to the hotel and upstairs. In the room he said, "Why don't you un paint yourself girl, I for one, would love to see just what you look like under that mask."

He thought for a minute she would refuse, but she smiled and went to the bath house in the hall and when she stepped back in the room his heart took a leap. The girl, while not a raving beauty was still a knock out. He said, "Now that's the way a beautiful woman should look."

Her face got red and she sat down on the bed. She asked him his name and he told her, He asked, "What's yours?"

The girl said, Bonny Joyweather. He came back with, "What a pretty name, where do you hail from?"

She said, "I grew up in Denver, but came down here on a whim and now here I am. Been down here one month and out of a job already."

Brandon was silent for a spell then asked her how she got here and she said, "I have a horse and an old buggy and they're both parked over at the livery stable. The horse cost me fifteen cents per day and the hostler lets me store my buggy for nothing."

Brandon asked her how much money she made over at the bar and she was quick to answer him. "Sometime I did pretty good, but mostly, I would go to my room upstairs with nothing. I refused to whore and that has always been a sore spot with ugly Joe the bartender. I won't go back and was thinking about leaving anyhow. Why don't we have some of that bottle and get to know each other?"

Brandon had never drank hard liquor in his life, but was willing to try. After one drink the two fell in bed and gave way to their passion. Brandon had been a virgin and was clumsy and had to be shown the way by the more experienced Bonny. This didn't detract from the sheer pleasure the two found in each other's body one iota. Brandon thought this was the most fun he had ever had without laughing and was up to a few more times before he said, "Enough girl." then went to sleep.

CHAPTER FIVE

Sometime, when two people fall in love neither one realizes it. This is what happened to Brandon and Bonny. They knew they were becoming good friends and this meant more to Brandon than sex in the long run anyhow. Bonny was a delight to be around, because she was upbeat about all aspects of life. Her down moments were restricted to, damn, I broke a nail and not much more. The two talked every night and day about what they wanted to do in life. Brandon told her about the money he had inherited from his friend Charley. He told her the instructions for finding the money was on the table next to Charley's will. It read something like a buried treasure map would.

Brandon didn't even look for the money until two months after Charley was buried. Then one day he was at loose ends and picked the paper up and followed the instructions on it. It told him to ride due west of the cabin until he saw three hickory trees in the first wooded area he came to and then ride east for one mile to a black berry patch and turn south again. After two hundred feet look for a hollow tree that had been struck by lightning. A big X marked the tree on his map and sure enough the packet of money was there.

Brandon had never had cash before and was appalled at how much there was. The packet was a stack of hundred dollar bills that Charley had inherited from his father when he passed away. Brandon had only cashed one of the big bills in so far and caused a bit of a stir in St. Louis, when he did. He still had most of the money from the sale of the mean horse that he got from his father's farm. The horse had never cottoned to him and attempted to bite, kick or stomp on him every time he got near it. So he just up and sold it for forty bucks. Horses were in great demand to pull barges up river with and the first person he talked to bought the nasty tempered beast for speculation. Brandon wished him luck.

The two young folks put their heads together about where and what they wanted to do with their lives. Bonny knew she liked this wild Appalachian turned cowboy and would follow him as long as he wanted her to. Brandon just didn't know if Bonny wanted to live her life on the trail like he did. He found out when he started making plans for moving on without her.

She said, "Listen Buster if you think you're going to leave me in this ass hole town you're crazy as hell. Where you go I go and that's that!"

Brandon thought to himself, boy, it sure is a good thing I want her to go with me.

Now on the trail together, they sorted themselves out. The buckboard was some kind of worn out and Brandon decided it wouldn't do, so they took it down to the livery and traded it in on a standard covered wagon and went to work to make a nest in the thing. A bed seemed pretty important to the two, so they searched for some kind of a mattress. The only thing they came up with was a feather bed that was twelve inches thick unless you laid on it and then your bones would set down on the floor boards and hurt like the devil by morning. Brandon solved that problem by a visit to the feed store and for a few cents he bought thirty gunny sacks that feed had been shipped in. After beating them half to death to get anything out that might have taken up residence, they laid them under the feather bed and they had a comfortable bed to sleep on.

The trading post owner must have thought he did the right thing to deserve such a wind-fall when the two shopped for everything needed to set up camp and housekeeping.

The horse that Bonny owned was a pretty good horse, but had never worked with another in her life so, Brandon and Bonny traded her for a matched set of mules called Jack and Joe. They were a good looking pair and took to their new owners readily, by braying at them whenever they approached them each day.

When the two finally got under way there was a bit of a crowd to see them off. The big bartender gave Brandon a, "why don't you go to hell" look and Brandon and Bonny both smiled at him as they pulled past him. Brandon hoped he never saw that man again, because if he did, there would be a killing and it wouldn't be Brandon that died.

Once out on the plains, they had fun and there were wild birds everywhere they looked. Brandon shot a pheasant for their supper and found it delicious. After supper they set around a small fire made of cow and buffalo chips and talked. Bonny said. "Can I ask you something please, Brandon?"

Brandon looked at her in surprise and said, "Why heck, I guess you can girl."

She asked, "Would you be able to show me how to draw and shoot like you do?"

Brandon secretly had a thrill to go up his back. He was pleased she wanted to emulate him and learn how to shoot.

He said, "Well, honey pot, if you really want to, I'll teach you and see how you do. You can use my gun for now and when you learn how, maybe we could get you your own."

Bonny was scared to death of the big colt forty-four at first and she took a long time getting accustomed to the weight of the heavy piece. Brandon unloaded the gun so she couldn't shoot her foot off or him and rigged his holster on her belt. He laughed at how big that gun looked on his little bitty girl. He told her to just wear it around for a few days and then he would show her how to load, cock and shoot the piece.

Within three days Bonny and the gun looked like they belonged together, so Brandon set her down around the fire that night and explained the workings of the most formidably six gun in the west, that turned weak men strong out here. He had her disassemble the colt and clean it and reassemble it. She got pretty good marks on this part of her training.

Next he taught her how to load the patch and ball and powder in the six cylinders. She had to work a long time at that and made Brandon slow down and give her more time to learn and practice what she had learned. She didn't give up however, in fact she doubled her efforts and by the next evening, she could load a cylinder in just a few minutes.

Brandon said, "When we get the chance we'll buy two new Smith and Wesson forty-fours.

They load with a shell that slips in the cylinder. But it's good that you're learning the old way."

CHAPTER SIX

The man looked mean, but he was trying to be nice and Brandon thought he knew why. This yo yo had eyes for Bonny and it just might get him shot.

They were in Clayton, New Mexico eating at the only place in town you could buy anything cooked. This person came out of the blue and sat down at their table. Brandon stopped eating and asked the stranger if he didn't mind, he and his friend would like to eat alone. The man got a mean look in his eyes, but apologized and left. Brandon forgot him and they finished their meal, paid and left for their hotel room. As they stepped out on the board walk the stranger was there once more. He stepped up and in too loud of a voice said, "Maybe you don't know who I am around here mister and it weren't polite what you said to me back there in that eating place."

Brandon said, "Then I apologize mister, and now would you excuse us please?"

The man grew red in the face at being rebuffed twice in a few minutes. He looked at the tied down holster holding a lethal looking forty-four and his gut turned to jelly and his stomach rumbled. He abruptly turned away and stomped back through the saloon door. Bonny wondered if that man knew how close he had come to death.

They were about to turn away and go to the hotel when at least twenty riders hit the main street coming from the west. They swung in at the saloon where there were a bunch of lathered up horses already tied up. The twenty or so riders hit the boardwalk at the same time and at a run almost tore the Saloon's bat wing doors off their hinges. Brandon and Bonny had to see what was going down in that saloon, so they reversed their course and went through the doors.

There was the loud mouth attending court with all the locals. He held a glass of whisky high and said, "We cut that Shipley barbed wire all to pieces. And we'll do it again right boys?"

The twenty riders stood there and waited. The loud mouth suddenly realized he was facing the same man who's barbwire he and his men had cut earlier that day and went for his gun. He never had a chance, the man who had to be the boss beat him to the draw by a mile and the loud mouth was dead on the way to the floor. About nine others in the bar went for their guns and even the two women in the Shipley bunch drew faster than they did. Soon there were ten bodies on the floor. Shipley said, "These men cut down ten mile of my fence and then attempted to shoot us. I'm Baran Shipley and if anyone cuts my wire they will receive the same treatment, the Bar-S ranch will not sit by and allow its fence destroyed."

The bunch turned and left.

Brandon and Bonny stood there and stared after the riders. They looked in each other's eyes and nodded in agreement. Barb wire was coming and there wasn't a thing to do about it.

CHAPTER SEVEN

"How about gold mining, do you think we could do some of that honey?" Bonny had been trying to come up with something that they could do together and that was the only thing that came to mind.

Brandon looked at his girl and was amazed that she came up with something that had always been on his mind. Since he learned to read he had a touch of gold fever and thought maybe they could do some of that. He had heard talk of riches beyond ones wildest dreams laying on the ground up on the Yukon River and told Bonny about it. Bonny came down with an extreme case of incurable gold fever, and got all excited and began making plans. She had gotten so good with Brandon's old cap and ball pistol that he found a gun shop in Santa Fe, where he bought two brand new Smith and Wesson Forty-Four's and another Henry Rifle. He found a belt and holster with a tie down strap for Bonny and she was ready to learn to shoot.

"Oh! My god that thing kicks like a mule Brandon." Bonny was massaging her bruised shoulder where the Henry that she held too loosely as she pulled a round off, had kicked the crap out of her, missing the target by a mile. Brandon made her hold the rifle tightly into her body and essentially become part of the rifle as she squeezed the next round off. Bonny did as he directed and she came within inches of the target and she didn't get hurt either. She became excited then and soon was hitting the target each time.

"Now hon, I want you to hold the gun with both hands at first anyway, later you will be able to use only one hand."

He wanted her to hit a target first and then he would teach her to fast draw and shoot at the same target, The big Smith and Wesson looked like a monster in her dainty hands. He thought maybe he should have bought her a smaller gun of some sort. Bonny was determined however and went at it like her life depended on it. The first round she fired scared the pee waddle doodle out of her. She shook her hands out and exclaimed they were asleep. Brandon explained that maybe she might be choking the gun a bit tight and she should relax her grip a bit. She looked at him and stuck her tongue out at him, making him laugh. She aimed once more and actually hit the tin coffee can dead center. She placed three more in the can and then missed the final round.

Brandon had Bonny pull and dry fire the pistol until she could draw fast.. At first she was clumsy and would have probably shot herself in the foot if she had any live ammo in the gun. She went for days until he figured she had a handle on drawing and shooting at a target.

Brandon said, "Ok, honey this gun is now loaded with five rounds and is now a deadly weapon and will kill whatever you shoot at, providing your aim is true."

He slid it in her holster and stepped back saying, "Before you pull the trigger, be satisfied in your mind, that you really want to shoot what you're aiming at."

Bonny drew the gun aimed and put a hole in a new can. She did this five times and hit the can each time. She was so excited that she ran to Brandon and hugged him.

Brandon said, "Girl you did great, now all you need do is get faster and you do that by drawing thousands of times and dry firing at any target you see."

Bonny went all day long drawing and dry firing and got a little better and faster each day. When Brandon thought the time was right he told Bonny to come and stand in front of him. He took all the bullets out of his gun and spun the cylinder to make sure it was unloaded. He had Bonny do the same. He told her, "We are going to draw on each other to see how you are progressing." He said. "You will draw first." Bonny began her draw and in a blur Brandon had her while her gun was still in her holster. She said, "Oh crap you beat me by a mile."

Brandon laughed and said, "Let me show you something."

"You told me you were going to draw with your eyes and body movement. That's called forecasting your action. You must learn to draw fast enough that your opponent has no inkling that you are drawing, now try again. This time concentrate on drawing the gun and do it fast and all at once."

Bonny came near beating Brandon the next time and soon she was more or less matching him draw for draw. He was so proud of her he hugged her this time. He had a real partner in their planed adventure to the Alaskan gold fields now.

CHAPTER EIGHT

"But what if the damn thing sinks Brandon, what do we do then?"

Brandon was tickled at Bonny as they drove the wagon into the hull of the Steamship Loggernought. The year was 1887 and gold had been discovered on the Yukon River. They had used some of Charley's hundred dollar bills to book passage from Seattle to Skagway Alaska, the last stop on the trail to the Yukon.

They had read about what was ahead of them and while it seemed romantic, there had been thousands climbing the trail and it had to be fraught with danger. He would have to hire some men to carry their disassembled wagon and goods up the Chillcoot Trail and he would reassemble it at the top. That's the way it should have worked, but it didn't. After a two week trip up through the inside passage they disembarked at the fort and found most people had gone on and there was no one to hire. Brandon simply took the mules and made pack mules out of them and stripped the wagon of its canvas. He bought one other saddle horse that named herself right off the bat by trying to bite him on the ass and was forever labeled "the bitch" for life. The bitch didn't try to bite Bonny, but never missed a chance to have a go at him. They packed everything they could and started up the Chilcoot Trail and found the going slow. It was June but all the snow wasn't gone yet and it froze each night.

When they broke out on top, there was a tent city there going full strength; with bars and whore houses set up in big tents. The whole scene was abhorrent to Bonny and Brandon and after gazing at the teaming city for a bit, they turned their mules off to the side and continued on their way.

Brandon looked for a camping place that was protected, but found none. He decided to make one on a hill that was timbered and had plenty of dead wood for fire. Brandon waded into the trees and found snow still two foot deep. He took his little axe and thinned some trees out and then took a shovel from Joe's pack and shoveled the snow out down to tundra and then built a fire. He limbed a long tree and made it into a ridge pole for the canvas from the wagon. It made a pretty good tent if you didn't mind a few air holes that is. Bonny took one look at the thing and declared she would do some sewing on it to close some holes up as soon as possible.

The snow become a berm around their camp and held the wind at bay. The temperature was warm in daytime but would freeze them at night. They had warm clothing and heavy coats and each other to keep warm at night. Jack and Joe the mules tried to get on top of the fire and would have if Brandon hadn't tied them up short. The camp fire was a nice thing and Bonny took on the job of gathering wood for it. There were a few problems of having to cook with melted snow for water at first, but Bonny was a trooper and never complained. They would be on the clear sweet Yukon River before long and she could have all the water her heart desired.

CHAPTER NINE

The beautiful Yukon was some sight to see. They were looking down on the little settlement of Whitehorse, that was swollen to four times its normal size and had more tents than houses. Brandon really didn't want to contend with all the hub bub, but he was shooting in the dark here and didn't have a clue what his next move should be. Bonny saved the day by being practical. She said, "We must build a raft out of wood and float down to the gold fields."

Brandon looked at Bonny and shook his head. He thought, boy and I thought she would be a problem and now she is the best asset he had. He went to her and asked, "Will you marry me Bonny and be my wife?"

Bonny didn't hesitate for a second. She just jumped into his arms and said, "Buster, it's about time. Yes I will marry you."

They got on their horses and rode into the teaming tent city and found a half drunk judge to say all the necessary words and rode back to camp Mr. and Mrs. Chedlow.

Brandon told Bonny they needed to travel downriver until they found a large stand of timber to build a raft from and she agreed. This raft must haul two mules, two horses and two humans with all their goods, down a few hundred miles of uncertain river.

Bandon had talked to different would be miners and come up with the conclusion they mostly were more in the dark than he was. He had every map of this part of the country that was available and they were at best, unreliable information sources. He and Bonny wanted to make it to Fairbanks, where they had heard a huge gold strike had just been made and the Yukon River didn't go to Fairbanks.

It turned right where the Tanana river joined with it for the run down to the sea. Somehow they had to get up the Tanana to Fairbanks. Some fellow told them there was steam boats running up to Fairbanks, but that was the long way around. They consulted their maps and saw that the mighty Yukon River came very close to Fairbanks before it wandered down to the conflux with the Tanana. Brandon decided he maybe could stop their raft there, off load and travel overland to the gold fields, which were on that side of Fairbanks anyway. Brandon reckoned since they had no rolling stock they could find ways overland.

The two Newlyweds went to work cutting down big spruce trees on the banks of the Yukon for their raft. The weather warmed and the days become longer and it didn't hardly get dark. The sun was shining at midnight one night and Brandon asked Bonny what day it was. She said the twenty-first of June the longest day of the year. The two were so enthralled neither went to sleep all night. This would be something they would tell their grandbabies, if they ever had any that is.

The big logs were green and heavy. A peeve moved them around, but Brandon wondered if they would float. He cut a five foot section and rolled it down to the water. The log sank until only just the top side remained dry. This stopped Brandon in his tracks. Those logs wouldn't hold any weight. Brandon hardly slept that night, because if the raft didn't work out they would have to give their plans up and return to the south.

Brandon set up in bed and yelled, "That's it!, the logs will loose their weight if we skin them."

He scared Bonny so bad that she grabbed her gun and cocked it. He looked at her and grinned saying, "Sorry about that baby, but I was stumped there for a bit and now every things OK."

Bonny put her gun down and hugged him as he explained they must skin the logs starting tomorrow and in a few days they would loose much of their weight and float high in the water.

The following day they skinned three of the twenty-four foot logs and wrestled them into position. The job of skinning become easier with practice and at the end of the following day twelve, twenty-four foot, twelve inch logs were skinned and drying in the warm sun. They went to work cutting smaller trees for the super structure, that would be an "A" frame on the rear half of the raft. The couple needed some place to get out of the weather when it turned foul. Hopefully they could land the raft during these periods and not proceed blindly down a river that might come to a great falls or go underground or a million other things.

Brandon made two steering rudders in case one broke. It would be catastrophic if that happened. He bored holes and installed two stanchions across the back two center logs to place the rudder arm in and it looked like it just might work. To keep the rudder from floating out of its place he leashed a small log across the top and the bottom of the two stanchions. He tied the raft together with rope and cross logs. It would still be a little limber but he figured that would be a good thing.

CHAPTER TEN

Launch day came on thirty June. The raft slid in the clear waters of the Yukon River and floated proudly, high in the water. As the day progressed the raft was packed with all the goods from the two mule packs and the canvas was secured as water proofing for the "A" frame. The Mules were a problem however and after some thought Brandon and Bonny decided to take them up river to White Horse and sell them. The round logs were too much for the two mules. Even though Brandon had taken great pains to level the animal end out, the mules refused to step a foot on the raft while the two horses didn't seem to mind one bit. Charley led the bitch right on and the two began munching hay that Bonny cut along the bank for them. There wasn't any concern from the horses about the rope pen they were contained in either.

The pair of mules brought three times the money they paid for them. the packs would have brought a fortune, but they needed them for the two horses when they deserted the raft and went over land to Fairbanks. They were sad about the mules, they had become good friends with the two.

Brandon untied the line and pushed the raft out in the current of the Yukon and jumped aboard, their die had been cast and they couldn't turn around now if they wanted to. For the most part, their hearts lifted up at the fantastic views that unfolded in a panoramic explosion with each bend in the river. The two horses even seemed to enjoy the scenery as well and old Charley nickered at them often.

They took care of keeping the raft clean and the biggest mess was the two horses crapping anytime they wanted. Bonny said, "We need a pooper catcher honey, that's what we need. All Brandon could think of was something to lay on the floor but they had nothing like that. He finally handed Bonny a bucket and she simply washed it into the water for now and maybe he'd come up with some hair brained scheme to catch their poop yet.

Brandon had been dozing at the tiller when he suddenly was scared half to death! The two horses were squealing and the raft had cocked up in the rear. Then he noticed they were hung up on a huge tree that had its root system washed out by some flood and was laying across their path. Brandon grabbed his bow saw and lit out for the front to calm the horses. Bonny beat him to them and held their halters and was calming the two down.

Brandon saw that if he cut the offending tree they would float free of it. It was twelve inches thick and was solidly attached to their raft. Brandon had to wade water up to his knees to get out to the tree. He figured if he began cutting the back side of the tree it would eventually break and go down stream with them. It almost worked that way, but when the top of the tree broke off and started downstream Brandon overbalanced and fell into the icy water. It took his breath away. He flung his saw up on the now un-submerged raft and swam to it and Bonny was there to help him aboard. He had never been that cold in his life. The sun sure felt good. The tree top he had severed from its trunk floated merrily alongside them.

On the twelfth day they rounded one more beautiful bend in the movie like view of the river and saw many canoes gathered on the beach below a log structure that could only be the Livengood Trading Post. This was to be their jumping off point for the trail to Fairbanks and its goldfields. Brandon maneuvered the raft over along the shore and Bonny jumped ashore and tied the line to a stump. The raft swung around and lay up on the bank slightly. Brandon went ashore and he and Bonny walked up the high bank to the trading post. The canoes on the beach they passed were full of different things and even one had a sleeping Indian in it. They both smiled at that. The door was closed on the log building in all probability to prevent entry to the ever thirsty mosquito. A hand drawn sign read COME IN. They walked through the door and confronted the owner, a three hundred fifty pound short round French Canadian. He smiled at the two and said, "Aie, someone make mistake here. Woman too beautiful for dis ugly country."

Bonny and Brandon took an instant liking for this man and shook his hand. He asked, "What you do out here where nothing is?"

Brandon told him he wanted to mine for gold and had plans to travel overland to Fairbanks and find some land to do that on. Frenchy, as he was called, shook his massive head and said, "Aie! I think you here wrong time of year. Trail to Fairbanks only good in winter time. Too many holes in tundra and when you step in one of them, you break leg and die in wilderness."

Brandon felt he had been dealt a dirty blow, no one had ever mentioned this to them before. He asked Frenchy, "How would two people get to Fairbanks now?"

Frenchy said, "Must canoe down Yukon and up Tanana river"

Brandon asked, "Where can we get a canoe that two people could move that way in?"

Frenchy grinned and said, "I see your raft come down and it's a good one. I trade you long canoe for your raft."

Brandon said, "Well, that sounds alright, but we have two horses that will not fit in any canoe."

Frenchy said, "I give you two hundred dollars for horses and saddles. They go overland this fall and become Fairbanks horses."

Brandon and Bonny stepped aside and discussed the offer. Bonny said, "I think Frenchy is giving us a good deal because he likes us and I feel we should do it."

Brandon went over and shook French's hand. Frenchy became all business then and counted out two hundred dollars and handed them to Brandon. He said, "Bring the horses around to back, you'll find a small barn and corral."

The canoe was a wooden affair made from birch bark and coated with spruce juice as the natives say, a concoction of spruce sap boiled from the tree itself. It was light as a feather and strong for its weight. When the canoe was completely loaded it still maneuvered with ease.

Brandon and Bonny went shopping at the trading post and spent most of old Charley and Bitches money on food, some clothing such as spare head netting and netting to cover them as they slept. Brandon had noticed a white trill canvas folded up on one of the shelves and asked Frenchy what it was? Frenchy said, "A wall tent for living in, you need eh?"

Brandon said, "You bet we do how much?"

Frenchy said, "For you thirty dollars."

Brandon didn't argue he just handed the money over and said, "We must be on our way, but first a couple of questions, how far is it to where the rivers join?"

Frenchy replied with, "Maybe three days float and you see big open water and you turn left and go up dirty river called Tanana to Fairbanks," he added, "Stay near shore and you find paddling much easier."

Frenchy followed them down to the canoe and stood watching them getting in it. He waved goodbye and yelled to them as they fast disappeared down river, "Don't forget to turn left or we find you in Russia maybe."

They all laughed at that remark.

CHAPTER ELEVEN

The canoe handled like a dream and all Brandon had to do right now was steer the craft. There was far too much beauty all around them to even bother with paddling. They saw Moose, Bear and one huge Porcupine along the banks and the conflux of the Yukon and Tanana hove in sight way too soon. As they entered the open water where the two mighty rivers met, the color of the water went from crystal clear to a muddy gray and then to a solid brown as they paddled up the Tanana. Both felt like turning and going back up the Yukon. They found the canoe did paddle easy up stream close to the bank, but the mosquitoes were relentless in pursuit of their blood and formed a cloud around their head. Brandon guided the craft out towards mid-stream until there were no cloud of the bugs around them. The current was somewhat harder to paddle against out there, but they were able to remove their head nets then.

There was no darkness at night on the tenth of July, in fact the sun never really set and at last they grew tired and looked for some place to camp for the night. Brandon saw an Island up ahead and steered to it. He reckoned camping here would serve two purposes; one, the dreaded Mossies didn't fly over water and two, bears don't really swim well. The two set up camp and used their wall tent to lay on and then pulled the remainder up over them. There were stumps of trees all over and the following morning Brandon chopped wood and built a fire where Bonny cooked some beans and bacon and what she loosely referred to as pone. It was a mixture of cornmeal and flour and fried in bacon grease. The stuff was delicious, but felt like a rock in their gut for most of the day. Both agreed no more pone for a while.

They were just getting ready to set out up stream, when they heard what sounded like a demon coming around the last bend. To their amazement a steam boat appeared in the distance. The boat wasn't moving fast against the six mile current and took a long time to reach them. When the huffing boat slowed to stop and maintained steerage. Brandon saw the name painted on its bow was "Fairbanks Queen" The captain came out on deck and yelled, "Need ride to Fairbanks?"

He was Indian and had a grin that reached from ear to ear. Brandon and Bonny looked at each other and then both nodded yes. The skipper motioned them to come on aboard. The two hopped in their canoe and paddled over to the boat. Brandon helped Bonny aboard and tossed her the line. The canoe fell in alongside the little steam ship and acted like it had found a new home. The captain introduced himself as Billy Carroll and that the fireman and him were the only two men aboard. He explained they would be stopping at different spots along the river to load wood and if they could afford a small fare he would enjoy their company. When asked what the fare was Billy laughed and said, "Twenty dollars for both of you, that OK?"

Brandon gave the twenty with a grin and said, "Thank you for stopping for us."

Billy grinned saying "Maybe you help load wood when we stop?"

Brandon thought damn, been snookered now, for sure. He laughed and said, " Only me, not Bonny."

Then Billy said, "That OK, you do her work too."

Brandon could see he would lose either way, so he nodded his head OK.

CHAPTER TWELVE

Fairbanks was a trading post along the Chena river with a few houses and thousands of tents. Miners were moving with purpose all over the place. Brandon and Bonny found it all a bit unsettling and decided to get the heck out of town as soon as possible. They parted company with Billy and continued their paddling up the slow moving Chena River.

They passed hundreds of mining sites and mountains of tailings from the mines turn the clear water of the Chena a rusty brown color. Soon the mining claims petered out and the Chena was drinkable once more, but tasted like iron. They found the feed creeks to be better water. They soon ran out of enough water to float the heavy canoe and decided to make a camp on the north bank of the Chena.

The first thing Brandon did was to cut some poles for the erection of the wall tent. He found two trees he could string a pole between for the ridge pole and the rest was easy. The side poles had uprights at each end and were held there by ropes to other trees. The Mosquitoes were horrendous. Bonny built little fires all over the place and soon the mossies pulled back to only a stray that didn't get the message that the air wasn't breathable any longer not even for the humans in camp. With red watering eyes the couple put their camp in order.

Brandon and Bonny began prospecting for gold signs in the close hills to the north. There were small streams everywhere and some looked promising and they took samples all the way up to where the stream become a trickle. It was on one of these streams that Brandon let go with a yell that made Bonny almost freeze with fear.

He said, "Gold! We've found gold.'

Bonny ran to him and looked in his pan. It held a handful of the yellow stuff. When Brandon poured it in a cloth sack it made a nice poke. The two went to work in earnest now and both panned gold until they were too tired to move and then fell into their bed exhausted.

Marauding bears were a pain in the butt for the two and more than one got shot for poking its nose in the tent looking for a meal and thought one of the humans might make a main course. Brandon shot one black bear that actually had

Bonny in its clutches and was about to run with her. Brandon always slept with his Forty-Four and placed two close shots at the base of the bears scull, killing it instantly causing Bonny to scramble out from under it. The two held each other and vowed they had enough gold and wasn't about to stay here another night.

They began packing up right then. Bonny had just had a close brush with death and all the gold in the world wasn't worth his wife's life. They broke camp, loaded the canoe and grabbed the bags of gold and Brandon was surprised at how much it weighed. They had mined a lot of gold and would stake this claim back at Fairbanks and always have it in case they needed it.

CHAPTER THIRTEEN

The heat waves were dancing as the two travelers looked across the salt flat and made them long for the cool Alaskan climate, they had so recently left. Brandon and Bonny had traveled back the way they had come, down the Yukon and up to Whitehorse, Canada.

Their gold had been worth a fortune and Brandon had cashed it all in at the trading post for a US government backed treasury warrant. The warrant was cashable by him or the bearer at any major bank in the USA. The trip up the beautiful clear Yukon River was pure pleasure with a lot of hard work involved for the two. They were happy to visit their friend Frenchy at Livengood Post and was happy old Charley was still there so Brandon could have one last visit. The trip down from Fairbanks had been in the canoe and when they passed the Fairbanks Queen they just waved and went on their way. Billy had the only sour look on his face they had seen then. Brandon knew he might have to load the firewood himself.

They spent most of the time cooped up in their cabin on the Alaskan Clipper, which was making its return to San Francisco down the inside passage.

The two were tired after making the two trips up the Chilcoot Trail. They needed to bring just the things they couldn't leave behind. Now they were crossing the great salt flats east of the Great Salt Lake in the Mohave Desert.

Brandon was thinking to himself that maybe they had made a mistake, when a wagon train appeared in the distance. At first the two thought it might be a mirage, but as the train grew closer, it proved to be the real thing. A rider detached from the train and rode out to meet them. The man was surly in his greeting to them, making Bonny swell up like a bandy rooster. He said, "What do you think you're doing out here on this desert by yourself?"

If he had grinned when he said it, it would have been taken a different way and things would have gotten better.

Brandon simply said, "We are doing just what the hell we want to mister and would kindly ask you to leave us the hell alone, while we do it."

The man puffed up like an adder and spouted off with, "Why don't you just go back the way you came, we don't need any strangers in this wagon train."

Brandon thought, the heat may have gotten to this fellow. Bonny beat him to the answer by saying, "Listen dumb ass, we're not even going your way, now leave us alone, please."

Brandon thought for sure the man was going to draw on Bonny. He held up his hand and said, "Mister, my wife will shoot you dead if you draw on her and if she doesn't then I will."

With great effort the man came back down to sanity and relaxed his stance. As he turned away his words rang out clearly, "We don't want you near our wagon train."

The two had no idea why this man was acting this way so continued on their way. As they passed the wagon train by, they noticed most of them were women and children and very few men. Brandon thought that very strange and discussed it with his wife. Bonny said, "I read in the San-Francisco newspaper about Polygamist. The man takes many wives and fathers many children with each woman. I bet that's what they are."

Brandon thought, I'll bet she is right and forgot about it.

CHAPTER FOURTEEN

The Great Salt Lake fell behind them as they traveled south along the Colorado River into Arizona. It was late fall, but still hot during the day but almost bitter cold at night. A fire was required to keep them warm unless they were in bed. The two horses they bought in San-Francisco were the best money could buy. Brandon named his horse Char, short for Charley and Bonny called hers Dumpling. The two horses tried to keep their noses in the fire all the time and had to be tied away from it. Two pack mules hauled their goods and were as faithful as Jack and Joe were and Brandon decided these two could carry the same names.

The Colorado River was a delight to the two. Brandon had bought some fish hooks and line and with grasshoppers for bait, he supplied Bonny with Rainbow Trout almost daily. They moved south at a leisurely pace, staying away from towns and spending days just lying in the sun and making love.

Brandon heard his wife say she was going in for a dip and would he like to come too, but he was almost asleep and declined. He heard Bonny scream and was up and running in an instant. He topped over the bank and saw his wife setting on the beach holding her leg. He ran to her and slid to a stop and asked what the matter was. Then he saw the snake as it swim away. It was a Water Moccasin. He had grabbed his Forty-Four at Bonne's scream and he used it to kill the snake.

He went to her and inspected where the snake had bitten her. There were two fang marks on her ankle and Brandon went right to work. He first carried her to their camp and grabbed some rope and tied a tourniquet near the top of her thigh. He hoped he had caught the poison before it reached that point. He found his skinning knife and cut an x in each fang mark and began to suck out the poison along with some blood.

Bonny had passed out from what he hoped was fright and not snake venom. The blood was mixed with some yellow stuff and he reckoned that was the snake venom. Bonny came to and asked him if she was going to die. He held her and told her not if he could help it. He was getting no more venom and knew he must allow some blood to flow or Bonny could loose her leg.

He let some pressure off the rope and the two wounds began bleeding. Brandon grabbed one of his clean shirts and ripped it to shreds. He put a folded piece over the two wounds and held pressure on them. Bonny began getting sick and throwing up. Soon she passed out once more. Brandon could only sit and pray his wife could fight the remainder of the venom off. The two wounds stopped bleeding and he put a bandage around her ankle. Her breathing was shallow and he began to worry that in spite of what he did she might die. He sat and held her and talked to her. Her leg started to turn blue and he knew he might loose his wife here. He cried tears for all the times they wouldn't have together and the loneliness he must face if she went away.

He dozed off and was woke up by Bonny saying, "Honey, I need a drink."

His wife looked like death to him and he hurriedly got a canteen and uncapped it. Bonny took only a small sip and didn't want anymore. Her eyes were bright and sad. She said, "I don't want to leave you my love, but this stuff in me is only getting worse. Please look up my mother in Denver and tell her I was thinking of her this day."

Brandon felt like he wanted to die right along with her He kissed her on the lips as she took her last breath. Brandon held Bonny so long that her body become cold. Then laid her on a blanket and covered her up. He felt like a great black hole had swallowed him up and he may never come out of it. The sun was still high, so he took a shovel off ole Joe's pack and with tears streaming down his face, dug a deep grave for Bonny. Leaving her wrapped in the blanket, he lowered her gently into her final resting place. He said what words he knew over her and covered her up. He found a packing crate and made her a cross and with his knife inscribed her name and the dates she lived on this earth.

CHAPTER FIFTEEN

Yuma, Arizona was a small town that Brandon stumbled into still full of grief over his wife's death. It stood near the Yuma Prison on the banks of the Colorado River that he had been following for so long. He never went in its waters after Bonny died.

The only relief Brandon found was in strong drink. He haunted the saloons and saw Bonny in almost every bar girls eyes, after he become drunk. He even tried to take one upstairs that reminded him of her, but he broke down and cried instead and caused the bar girl to kick his butt out of her room. Brandon went down and slept with old Char and Dumplings. They seemed to be happy with his company.

There were plenty of chances for trouble but, Brandon was too sad to even answer a challenge and soon was laughed at by the few other gun slicks in town. He just bought a bottle and went to his horse friends down at the stable.

He wasn't looking after himself well at all and more or less become the un-official town drunk. The marshal looked at this with some trepidation, because he knew this man, and something had rendered him useless as a human. He had seen Brandon draw his gun so fast it was out before the other man's left the holster.Brandon had put the barrel between his eyes and stopped a killing cold. He made up his mind that he just couldn't stand to see Brandon this way any longer. When Brandon got up and washed his face in the horse trough, the marshal stepped up and said, "There's coffee in my office and this is no invite so come on son."

Brandon didn't really want to go, but he knew better than to fight the law, so it would be the best thing to let him play his hand and see what develops. He meekly followed the marshal over to his office and inside. The marshal poured two gigantic cups of steaming coffee. He sat one in front of Brandon and said, "Drink up son you need it."

Brandon looked at the marshal with bloodshot eyes and said, "I like sugar in my coffee sir, if you have any."

The marshal suddenly grinned and opened a desk drawer and pulled out a cloth bag of sugar and set it on the table. He got a spoon from the same drawer and slid it across the desk top.

With a hand that shook so bad that some sugar wound up on the desk, Brandon sugared his first cup of coffee in two months.

The marshal said, "What happened son? What made you this way? You're destroying yourself and I intend to find out why."

Brandon took a sip of the coffee and felt like he needed to throw up, but focused on what the marshal had just said, then instead of throwing up, he said, "My wife Bonny was snake bitten and died in my arms up on the Colorado River a few months ago."

The Marshal shook his head and replied with, "Oh, hell man I didn't even know you were married and I am so sorry for your loss. When did you get married."

Brandon said "We were married up in Whitehorse, Canada last spring."

The marshal asked him if this girl was known to him and Brandon replied, "She was the girl I took from a saloon up in Dalhart, Texas."

The Marshal said, "I knew her and I was there when you did that. That was one of the nicest bar girls I ever saw. I'm still sorry for your pain and I'm damn sure gonna do something about it."

He reached in his desk drawer and took out a Deputy badge and tossed it to Brandon. Brandon picked the heavy badge up and turned it around in his hand. He raised his eyes up and looked in the marshal's and said, "At one time I wanted to become a law officer, but I don't believe I can do the job now sir."

He had tears rolling down his face. Evan Donald Lansing, Marshal, almost succumbed to tears as well. This boy was at the end of a very short rope, and nowhere to run.

Evan said, "Raise your right hand son."

Brandon did as he was told. "Do you swear to uphold the laws of the United States of America and to defend the constitution against all who might attempt to bring it down or tear it apart?"

Brandon was silent for a short space and then said, "You bet I will sir, with or without a badge."

Marshal Lansing said, "You are now a legal law officer and my Deputy. Get yourself cleaned up and sobered up and report tomorrow morning for work. You be here at five AM, because I have to ride over into California and bring a prisoner back to Yuma prison."

Brandon needed to get out of here real quick before he up-chucked all over his new boss and his new boss knew it too. Evan released him without a word and Brandon took off and made it to the ally before he brought up all the coffee. He wanted a drink, but law officers didn't get drunk did they? He went over to the hotel and rented a room. The desk clerk started to deny him one until he saw the gleaming badge on Brandon's chest. He had thoughts that maybe the badge wasn't real, but why take a chance and hadn't the man paid with a hundred dollar bill.

The bathhouse was run by a funny little Mexican by the name of Loony. Loony poured hot water in a tub and Brandon had his first hot bath in many months, no wonder folks gave him a wide berth on the street. His other baths had been at night in the horse trough. He wore clean clothes and was sure to put his badge on the new shirt.

He was hungry as a half-starved Coyote. He went to a steak house and was embarrassed that four bites of steak filled him up. He apologized to the waitress and left her a dollar tip, that probably caused a small inflation wherever she lived.

Back in his room, he fell in bed and didn't wake up until daylight filtered into the room. He got up and it hit him then, he wanted a drink more than he wanted life and had full intentions of finding one down at one of his stashes in the stable. Then he saw his reflection in the mirror and was appalled that the gaunt man in there was in fact him. He took in the badge on his chest and thought of Bonny then sat down on the bed and cried for her loss. He finally pulled himself together and went down for coffee. He had to stick this one out or he was lost, and that was against Gods wishes; according to the bible anyway.

He couldn't eat any breakfast, so went to the marshal's office. The door opened readily and the marshal was sitting at the desk. He looked up and said, "Good morning Deputy, I trust you had a good night's rest?"

Brandon answered with, "Well, yes I guess I did at that marshal."

Brandon asked him what his job was today and the marshal said, "Just hold the fort down and try to do some healing up if you can, a few days and you will be the man I remember."

The hours dragged ever so slowly, making him want a drink in the worst way, but the marshal's words came back each time his resolve weakened. Brandon was absolutely convinced he was going to die if he didn't get a drink. From one minute to the next for hours he went from, "I've got to have a drink", to remembering what the marshal had said to him.

Lunch time came and there was a knock on the door. When it opened an elderly lady stuck her head around the edge of the door and smiled at him. She said, "Good day to you Deputy, I sure hope you are hungry because I cooked some good food up just for you. My name is Mavis and I am Evan's wife of too many years to count."

She bustled about the desk and set what looked like a fine home cooked chicken dinner on the make do table. The aroma from the food was almost too much for him. His stomach heaved at the same time his mouth watered. With a super human effort he began eating. Mavis left him to it with the parting words, that she would pick up the empty plates later. Brandon had a hard time of it, but he made a reasonable dent in the large meal. He felt better after eating and thought maybe he might survive after all.

Brandon was startled by a man bursting through the door and excitedly telling him there was trouble over at the saloon and he should put a stop to it, or someone would be killed for sure. Brandon thought to himself, well, here is where I find out if I can still cut it. He stood and followed the local man to the saloon across the street.

Brandon stepped into the saloon and stopped, once inside he let his eyes adjust to the dim light. He saw Ralph the bartender being taunted by a gunman, the same one Brandon had refused to accept a challenge from earlier. The man had a deadly look about him and had in fact killed a few unfortunate wantabe gunman across three states.

Brandon bellied up to the bar and looked at his friend Ralph and asked, "How are things Ralph?"

Ralph locked eyes with him and there was a warning in them. The gunslick turned towards Brandon and sneered, "Well if it ain't the town drunk sporting a badge, now that takes the big prize don't it?"

The man had the rest of the noon crowd's attention then. He fully faced Brandon and spouted off once more, "Can you use that forty-four on your hip mister, or is it something you only play with?"

Brandon stood in silence for a few seconds and then in a low voice said, "Mister you are on the wrong track, My wonderful wife Bonny died up river from snake bite and I may have dived into a bottle for a spell, but please be aware that if you pull leather on me, I will kill you. So why don't you just walk out of here with your life still intact and call it even."

The man was a bully and had never seen anything from this drunk that might be of any harm to him. He went for his gun and in a blur Brandon had his gun out, while the bully was halfway through his draw. The man died with surprise written on his face. A gasp went up from the galley of saloon drinkers.

Ralph said, "Brandon you just outdrew and killed the top gunman in Yuma, do you know that."

All Brandon said was, "He made the choice Ralph."

Brandon turned and walked back to the marshal's office. He took pin and ink and wrote Evan a note. It said, "Thank you Marshal for saving my life." He took the badge off and laid it on top of the paper and walked out. He had Char and Dumpling saddled and packed and was out of town in one hour flat. He took no whisky with him.

CHAPTER SIXTEEN

Denver was too loud, and had too many humans, too many horses pulling rigs and mostly made him yearn for faraway places. Brandon sat his horse Char and gazed at the teaming city wondering how he would find one person in all that mess.

Her name had been Joann Joyweather at some stage, but could be anything now, seeing as how she could have remarried after Bonny's father had died, before Bonnie left home and went to Dalhart, Texas to seek her fortune. Tears sprang to his eyes remembering how she died.

The only thing Brandon knew for sure to do was ask anyone he met if they did or ever know a Joann Joyweather and the best place was the drinking establishments of Denver. He also knew there was a passel of trouble in every one of them. He thought about going unarmed, but on second thought, figured he might be recognized and gunned down by some hot head who didn't even see that he was unarmed. He wore his gun and went to work.

The Western Barn was a new breed of big saloons. It had huge rooms for gambling and even had live bands and orchestras playing with well-known singers as they performed nightly. The clientele was mostly local and tended to be middle age persons and couples mixed with some singles.

Brandon installed himself at a corner table where he had a clear view of the street and the huge bar as well. The table waiter took his order of a beer and a menu for food. When they came, Brandon asked the waiter his questions and received a negative answer. He figured maybe he had better get used to that.

He caught the attention of a man at the bar. The man was a gunslick and after a while made his way over to Brandon. He seemed friendly however and Brandon asked him to park himself. The man said, "I know you hombre, I saw you over in Dalhart one time, I just can't recall your name."

There was no menace in his voice, so Brandon held out his hand and introduced himself. The man returned his handshake and said, "I'm Doc Jones and I'd like to buy your next beer. I've never seen anyone as fast as you on the draw and I would much rather be your friend than your enemy."

Brandon smiled and said, "You have it my friend and as far as a beer, one's my limit and if you hear my story you will understand why."

Doc came back with, "I know some of the story, but if you need to tell it, I'll listen."

Brandon started to like this man and didn't miss the fact that Doc reminded him of a younger Charley. They both knew he needed a friend and right now it couldn't be a woman, simply because every woman reminded him hauntingly of Bonny. The two gunman found common ground in the fact that neither were really born killers and only answered a challenge that could kill them, if they did not answer it.

Doc, born Dannion David Jones, grew up in the suburbs of Memphis, Tennessee. He had two sisters older than him and they both married before he turned twelve years old. His mother and father were getting on in years when smallpox took them away and left young Dannion to fend off an over loving aunt and uncle that laid claim to him the minute his parents were in the cold ground. As far as Dannion was concerned he was fast becoming a man and started to get involved with guns.

When he turned thirteen he found an old war pistol in the attic where his tiny room was. He had been rummaging through the things that had accumulated over the years and almost gave everything away when he yelled in excitement at finding the gun and military holster with US burned on it.

His uncle came up the stairs at a run when he heard Dannion's outburst. Doc heard the clump of his uncle's footsteps and dove for his cubby hole and gently shut the door to the attic. He was laying in bed with a book when his red faced uncle burst into his room.

His Uncle Buster wanted to know what he had yelled about and Doc had lied like hell. He said, "At this funny book Uncle."

His uncle turned with a curse and clumped back down the stairs. Dannion was relieved especially when he noticed the book was his history book from school and he was holding it upside down.

Dannion strapped that pistol on every chance he got and it wasn't long before it felt a part of him. He had no clue how to load the thing, even though there were bullets, patches and powder in a bag with the gun. His entire thirteenth year was spent in school and learning how to fast draw that old pistol. By the time he turned fourteen he was getting fast and needed to load the gun and shoot a target.

While walking home from school each day he would stop at the stock yards and climb on the fence and watch the cowboys cut stock out for slaughter. One cowboy spoke to him each time he saw him and began talking to him some. Dannion noticed the cowboy wore a gun on his hip just like the one he found in the attic of his uncle's house. Doc asked him about his gun one day and the cowboy pulled it out and handed it to Doc. His eyes opened wide when he saw the way Doc handled the piece. He said, "Boy, you have had one of those in your hands before haven't you."

Doc bobbed his head and came back with, "I have one just like it, but don't know how to load it."

Over the next three months the cowboy taught him how to load and shoot the gun. The cowboy was fairly fast on the draw, but Doc could out draw him two times over. One day when he went to the stockyards to see his friend, he was told the cowboy had moved on. Doc was devastated for days, because he had thought they were becoming friends and the man didn't even say goodbye.

One thing led to the other and when he was fifteen, his Uncle Buster died from a massive heart attack and his Aunt, being younger than her recently departed husband, set her seductive sights on the strapping young man she had raised up. This scared Doc so bad, he packed up his few clothes and his gun and hit the railroad west. He probably wouldn't have survived a day without his ole pistol. He didn't hesitate for one second to pull down on anyone who threatened him in anyway. No one else had guns in the hobo jungles he spent time in and he found as long he stayed separated from the rest, he was left alone.

Doc had no skills except his gun and there were no jobs readily available for a sixteen year old gunslick. He got work in Kansas City shoveling out stables at the race track. The pay wasn't much, but he got a room to sleep in and three meals each day at the race track mess hall. He became friends with all the resident horses and knew them by name.

One of the trainers noticed his expertise with the horses and offered him a pay hike if he could learn to ride and exercise them. Doc took to his new job like rain to dust and over the next year learned everything he could about horses. He bought one with a western saddle for the paltry sum of fifteen dollars from a passing wagon train. It seemed the last owner had died in the saddle and the horse was a hindrance to the wagon train. He felt like a million dollars on that horse and promptly left the employment of the

Kansas City race course and moved west along with any wagons going that way.

He hunted game and traded it for everything he thought he could use, and donated what he couldn't use to the families that were having hard times on the trail. By the time he reached western Kansas he had a great outfit and a name for his horse. He called her Faith because she was devoted to him and nickered to him each time he approached her.

He and Faith had moved south into the Texas panhandle for the winter and back north when the weather got too hot down south.

Doc told Brandon he had to shoot four men in self-defense and he pulled his gun out and showed Brandon the four notches on the wooden handle. Brandon noticed the gun was a Forty-Four patch powder and ball war pistol.

Brandon knew it was his turn to talk, so he began and an hour later he was in tears again and made Doc feel sadder than he had ever felt.

Brandon and Doc become good friends and riding partners over the next four months and were a common sight wherever they went. Both took jobs riding the feed lot at the Denver slaughter yards. The pay wasn't good, but the two had fun cutting the stubborn range cows and dodging their horns. Faith was one of the most sure footed horses on the lot and all the other cowboys tried to buy her from Doc but there would never be any chance of that. Doc was a "funny, have a good time" type of person and made Brandon laugh a lot at his witty sayings. This was just what a doctor would have ordered for the broken hearted man.

CHAPTER SEVENTEEN

Brandon knew his side kick wasn't a wealthy man by any stretch and needed to come up with something better than forty bucks a month job for the both of them.

When Bonny had died, he thought he would never want to return to his mining claims on the Chena river above Fairbanks, but when he thought of the money he and Bonny had extracted from the ground, he began to have different thoughts about it. One day out of the blue, he approached his buddy about mining gold in Alaska and to his surprise, Doc was very interested. Brandon told him the story of him and Bonny going and coming back with a good bit of scratch between them and his partner showed he had a bit of gold fever in his soul. He simply asked, "When do we go pard?"

It was March and too cold to be in Alaska, but now would be the time to start preparations.

We'll need a large canoe to haul our gear up there. Bonny and I left a lot of gear on the claim so we can hope no one has stolen the stuff.

Doc was quieter than normal and caused Brandon to stop talking. The two had been Pards long enough to know when the other had something on his mind. Doc said, "You know, I've been thinking about all the trouble we will have taking a steamship up to Alaska and then all the God awful work of dragging all our gear up that trail you describe and the biting bugs, which this cowboy hates and I live in fear of bears too. Why not stay closer to home and go look for gold in the California gold hills north of San-Francisco. It's not near as far as that Chena river and we could be there in a few days, if we left right now."

Brandon looked at his friend in amazement. He had been having the exact same thoughts. He would have been in total misery following in his dead wife's footsteps all the way to and from Alaska and wasn't looking forward to the trip at all. Brandon grinned and shook Doc's hand and said, "Let's git our gear packed pard, because California here we come."

Guns, Gold and True Love

CHAPTER EIGHTEEN

Well, If you raise the mill to the top before you start the engine it might not choke the thing down. The two miners were using the latest method to extract gold from solid rock. They were hard rock mining. The month was June and Doc Jones and Brandon Chedlow had been doing this same type of mining with different measures of success. They almost always made a living and always remained friends no matter what. Neither was greedy and both were reasonable good cooks, so the years had rolled along comfortably.

They discovered gold back in eighty-six high up in the Cascade Range, north of Redding, California. The two had prospected for years finding only enough gold to keep their interest up until back in the spring of eighty-eight. They had gone where both figured there would be no chance to find gold and one day Doc let go a yell that galvanized Brandon into action. He pulled his Forty-Four and went to his friends rescue only to find him dancing about like a looney person holding a big rock in both hands. Brandon holstered his gun and grinned at his funny friend.

Doc chortled that their troubles were all over now and handed the rock to Brandon. The thing weighed a ton for its size. There was a vein of gold half an inch wide running right through its center. The two started looking around and found many more of the same. All they had to do was learn how to crush the rock and there would be the gold. Brandon took two rocks and banged them together and there it was, a hand full of gold. The two wore their hands out and quit. There had to be an easier way. They decided to take what gold they had broken from the rocks and go to Redding and stake their claim.

"Will this thing actually work? Brandon asked.

The man at the counter said, "Well, the instructions says it will, but no one around here has tried it."

The machine he and Doc were looking at was called a hammer mill and was a marvel that was supposed to break the rock into dust and release the trapped gold from within. It had a gasoline motor on it and neither had ever seen one before and the thing was scary according to Doc. The motor was a one cylinder foot start washing machine motor affair. Its main source of power was a flywheel that must have accounted for three quarters of its weight. A belt of canvas ran off the flywheel and operated the hammer.

Both of the miners had heard these odd machines were powering something called an air machine that the Wright Brothers back east were experimenting with. Doc just couldn't see any future in a flying machine that made such a god awful noise as this one did. The thing was cantankerous to start and died all the time when the rocks it ingested were too big for it. The hammer had to be raised to its fullest up stroke and then they could start the engine. If the rocks weren't too massive for the hammer, it would continue to bust rocks until the thing ran out of gas.

It was hard work, but the two extracted a bunch of gold from their mountain side. The vein ran back into the mountain and soon they had a cave that had to be supported by timbers inside. This was a lot of work and required skills neither really had, so they learned as they went. The timbers had to be cut down the mountain side where the timber line began and snaked up to the mine by the two horses.

One day Brandon stopped in his tracks and surveyed what they had done so far and it was like the first time he really saw it. They had made a perfect place to live back in that mountain.

When Doc saw his friend standing in wonderment, he stopped beside him and asked, "What's the matter old son?"

Brandon asked, "What do you see here that we have done, Doc?"

Doc looked at his partner like his spark plug had jumped out or something, then said, "Well, we damn sure got us a gold mine started that's for sure."

They were both silent for a spell then Doc exclaimed, "Damn pard, I see what you mean, that is one hell of a secure place back in our mine and we should move in there and not have to fight these wild critters out here." (There had been some close calls with Grizzlies since they had become miners.)

Doc said, "I made up my mind the last time one of those critters made a play and tried having me for dinner, that one more time and I would be gone and go somewhere, where bears don't exist."

Brandon was tickled at his friend, but more or less felt the same. These huge mountain bears were a scary lot and even the horses weren't safe and both knew it. Many a night had been wasted on bear watch that wore the two to a frazzle.

Brandon and Doc began to build a bear proof, if there was any such thing that is, stable on the side of the mine shaft that now would become their home. The two horses were turned into their new place and nickered their agreement. A bear could still crawl over the seven foot fence and get to the animals, but would make so much noise that it could be shot before doing any harm. At least there would be plenty of bear rugs for the floor of their new home.

CHAPTER NINETEEN

This was the third saddest day of Brandon's life. His best friend had died in his sleep and now Brandon was burying him near the mine he loved. Doc had come down with a cold that seemed to get worse each day. Brandon wanted to take him to a doctor down the mountain, but Doc said no, "If God wants me, he will take me and I don't feel up to no trip anyhow."

Before he died, he had signed all his possessions over to Brandon and told him he had no living relatives he knew of.

The place couldn't hold Brandon after his friends death. He packed all his personals up, closed and locked the massive door to the mine shaft home and rode down the mountain towards the town of Redding.

Doc's horse was heavy with gold and his saddle bags were half full as well. They had a good season and he would never want for money for the rest of his life. He was rusty with his fast draw and began drawing and dry firing his Forty-Four as soon as he left the mine.

Brandon was approaching forty years old and felt it in his bones, but he was still a striking hunk of manhood and in town, turned many a ladies head as he rode down the street. He stopped at his bank and commenced to carry sack after sack of gold inside. The banker was the only one in town that handled gold. He was honest with his dealings with miners from the mountains and there was no question he ever cheated these hard working people. He made 10% for his trouble and deposited the rest in a bank account in the miners name. He shook Brandon's hand and asked about Doc. Brandon silently handed him the paper work the two friends had drawn up when it looked like Doc wasn't going to make it. The banker was devastated over Doc's death and stated he would miss Doc's humor. Brandon said, "Yes, we all will."

It had been a long time since Brandon had entered a saloon, but he needed a drink and that was the only place to get one. He bellied up to the bar and ordered a beer. The bar maid was a striking lady of maybe twenty-five years and very friendly. She served his beer and retreated to the far end of the bar. Brandon needed to talk to someone so he motioned to her and when she came to him he asked if he could buy her a drink. She leveled a look at him and said, "I'll be off in a few minutes and then you can buy me a drink kind sir."

Her smile lit up the room and made Brandon feel warm inside. He said, "That's a date mam."

He took his beer and walked to a table, hooked a chair with the toe of his boot and sat down. He looked around the saloon then and took note that there were some pretty rough characters hanging out here.

The lady from the bar was true to her word and came to his table, he jumped up and held her chair. He sat back down and asked her what she would like to drink? She said. "I'm not a real drinker so I'll have sassafras tea."

He said, "I'll be right back, now don't you disappear into thin air please."

The lady smiled and said, "Don't you worry, sir I'll be here when you return."

They locked gazes and held it longer than maybe they should. Brandon finally broke off his gaze and rushed to the bar. He came back with a glass of sassafras tea and a new beer for himself. He introduced himself to her and waited for her to do the same. She said, "My name is Naundas Evelyn Whitiker."

They moved into conversation with an ease Brandon hadn't had with a woman since his wife

Bonny died over twenty years ago. He told her his life story, leaving the gunslinger part out for the present anyhow. Naundas was in tears when he reached the recent death of his friend Doc.

She told Brandon that she had seen the two of them around town and was really sorry he had passed on. The two talked until closing time at two AM and went for coffee at the diner around the corner. Both were reluctant to part company. Finally Naundas said, "I live by myself and while I don't normally take any man to my place, I feel such a strong appeal towards to you that I can't help myself."

Her face was crimson and her eyes were on the floor. Brandon knew this was a hard thing for this girl to do. He said, "I'll sleep on the floor so let's go."

CHAPTER TWENTY

That had been four months earlier and now they were man and wife. The courtship had lasted only a week before they both knew they were soul mates and stuck together like glue. Now they were sitting and looking down on the great city of Denver. They had ridden over the Rocky mountains and camped wherever they liked. Game was plentiful and water was everywhere they looked. Sometime the altitude would make their breath short, but soon they would ride down in a valley and breathing become not so hard. Brandon soon realized he had gotten lucky when he found Naundas. She was loving and was learning how to cook under his tutelage When they had first got together he swore that Naundas couldn't keep from burning water. Now she could put a pretty mean meal together.

The main purpose of them visiting Denver once more was to try and locate his dead wife's mother and inform her of her daughter's death.

He had had no luck before, but thought he'd give it one more try. He went first to the Denver Record and posted an ad for the lady in the name of Joann Joyweather. It read; "If Joann Joyweather reads this notice please reply to this newspaper, there is an urgent message for you".

Brandon didn't really expect any response, so he was shocked when he showed up at the paper office the following day to find no other than his unknown mother-in-law waiting with wringing hands. She was old and white headed, but looked in good health.

Brandon asked, "Mam. are you the mother of Bonny Joyweather?"

The lady looked at him and replied with, "Yes I am, and who are you ?"

Brandon said, "I was married to your wonderful daughter until a water moccasin bit and killed her a few years back. She is buried along the Colorado River north of Yuma, Arizona."

Tears sprang to his eyes as the memories come flooding back. Mrs. Joyweather began to cry and sat down on a chair and put her head in her hands. Brandon sat beside her and put his arm around her. They both had a good few minutes of grieving and suddenly she rose and said. "Thanks for coming and telling me." Then she was gone.

Brandon was shocked, but now understood why his wife had gone off on her own at such a young age.

Naundas said, "Don't let it bother you honey that woman is an old whore, believe me I can tell."

Brandon looked at his wife and said, "I believe you are right." He decided to forget all about it and enjoy his new wife as much as she would let him.

CHAPTER TWENTY-ONE

The very next morning Brandon told his wife, he had a hankering to return to his Appalachian mountain home. He had left there while he was still a boy and still owned the place. He had been gone a long time and didn't even know if the places he owned were still standing or not.

Brandon and Naundas took their time and enjoyed the turn of century in America that was becoming a thriving nation. There were wonders to see that one never dreamed of and the most wonderful was the availability of ice cream in almost every town they came through. Brandon thought he just might get fat eating it every time they got the chance. They saw their first movie in Kansas City the characters were jerky and animated and there was no sound, but they enjoyed them so much they went each time there was a new theater in their path. They found the new stores to be a delight and Naundas went shopping and made Brandon swear she was going to force them right out of their wagon and have them walking along behind the thing.

CHAPTER TWENTY-TWO

Brandon was dumb struck! Where Charley's old cabin had sat was now occupied by a relatively new house. There was not one piece of Charley's cabin remaining. He and Naundas sat and looked at what was going on. There were three little kids playing in a sand box in the front yard and then a woman came to the door and shielding her eyes with her hand looked at them and smiled.

Brandon moved the team closer to the house and the woman came down to the white picket fence and said, "Hello there can I help you folks?"

Brandon said, "Well maybe you can tell me what you are doing building a house on a piece of land I hold the deed to,"

Brandon thought the woman was going to faint right there. She said in a squeaky voice, "Oh no you must be Brandon Chedlow."

Brandon said, "I most certainly am and who might you be young lady?"

The girl said, "I am Shelly Willow and we are related somewhere way back."

Brandon didn't want to be a harsh man, so he suggested they might get down and go inside and discuss this problem. The girl didn't hesitate for a second. She said, "Oh do come on in, I suppose you own this place anyhow."

The three children had by this time gathered around and were fast winning Naunda's heart. They were clean and mild mannered intelligent small kids and were instantly attached to Naundas. They escorted her right into the house. Brandon noticed the house was immaculately clean with furniture that was worn, but clean and comfortable. He thought he recognized Charley's old leather couch, but didn't say anything about it. Shelly put coffee on and asked them to be seated in her dining room. Brandon noticed there were whatnots all over the place and some of them looked expensive. He asked Shelly who made them and her face grew red with embarrassment, as she admitted it was her doing.

Brandon wanted to hear how this all came about and gave Shelly a chance to explain. Shelly said, "My father heard about the death of his brother in law from the flu and moved here when I was a baby. He took over his brother-in-laws place and we lived there almost twenty years. I married and needed a place to raise my children. We had no idea this belonged to you, but later some words were whispered that it did in fact belong to you, but by then my husband had built this house and it was too late. My husband took off on me two years ago after the birth of my youngest. He wrote me once from Amsterdam and told me he would be able to send money now that he was a Merchant Mariner. The next letter I got told me that he had died when the ship sank in a storm. Twenty men lost their lives on that boat so now I'm a widow."

She was weeping softly, causing Brandon and Naundas to feel sorry for her. He asked her how she had survived since and she waved her hands around her at the many whatnots and said, "I take these down to a lady in Harrisonburg, where she runs a small shop and she sells them for me on a fifty-fifty basis. There's always a check waiting on me when I go down."

Brandon asked, "What about your parents, are they still living?"

Shelly said, "My father passed away three years ago and my mother still lives at the old place. I tried to get her to move here but she won't do it. She blames it on the children, but I think she is just set in her ways and will die there."

Brandon told Shelly he and Naundas were going out and have a talk concerning her predicament and would return shortly. He saw a cloud come over her face and said, "There will be no decision to kick you out or anything like that Shelly, so rest easy."

Shelly ran to him and said through tears, "Oh thank you, thank you." The three children run to the two and got in on the hug as well.

Outside, Brandon said, "Well, what a strange twist of fate this is. I think I want to help these people not hurt them, what do you think honey?"

Naundas said, "If you do what I think you're going to do, it will make a big difference in these four people's lives. I'm right there with you darling."

Brandon said, "Right, let's do it."

They sat at the table and Brandon told Shelly his story; starting back in Charley's time and finally ending here where he discovered this delightful family living on a piece of land that he held title to. He said, "I have been very successful at making money in my life and there is one thing I can do for you and that is pass on my friends legacy to you and these children. When Charley died he gave directions to his stash of money he had received as an inheritance from his father when he died. It was a stack of one-hundred dollar bills and they are still in my saddle bags in the wagon, I'll go get them while you two ladies visit."

Five minutes later he came back in and laid a canvas pouch on the table. The thing was a bit raggedy after all these years and smelled like money. Shelly was taking real short breaths, almost as if, she took a deep one all this might disappear. The three children were quiet and had saucer eyes as Brandon removed the money from the pouch. He began to count it. When he reached one-hundred he pushed that stack out of his way and began another. He counted sixty-seven in this stack. There were $16,700.00 dollars there and had Shelly holding her breath now. Brandon pushed both stacks over to her and said, "A gift from me and Charley, may he rest in peace.

Tears were streaming down Shelly's face now and the three children went to her and hugged their mother. Brandon hugged Naundas and had a warm feeling in his heart.

CHAPTER TWENTY-THREE

The Chedlows left Shelly Willows house with a full heart and good weather to travel in. Both agreed they wanted to see the ocean. Neither had before and now they could afford it. They came up to a recently installed fence and gate. There was a young boy standing beside a sign that read, "Toll way, pay here". Brandon saw the boy had a rusty old shotgun in the crook of his arm. Brandon stopped the team and asked the boy, "What in hell is this?"

The boy smiled and said, "This here be a toll road across me property mister."

Brandon was amused at the seriousness of this lad. Brandon said, "Well, what if we don't want to pay you your dollar? Is there another way around?"

The boy said, "Ai sir there is, ye just turn down that trail over yonder and go three miles to the end of me fence and turn right and go one mile then turn right again and go another three miles and ye be back on the same trail."

Brandon and Naundas were tickled by this time and knew they had been successfully snookered by this Irish boy. Brandon took out a silver dollar and flipped it to the boy who caught it perfectly with one hand. He said, "I be thanking ye mister and ye ave permission to proceed."

Brandon thought, the Irish just might have a place in this country after all.

Whatever it was that was coming towards them was scaring the bejebbers out of their team. The two mares stopped in their tracks and backed up and peed all over the tongue of the wagon. Brandon told Naundas to get down from the wagon in case the two excited horses took off. He ran to their heads ignoring the hub bub approaching them from the front. He grabbed the two mares bridles and talked soothingly to them. The apparition finally wound to a stop a hundred feet from them and went quiet.

The horses calmed right down then, so Brandon turned to the noisy piece of machinery and saw there were three people sitting in an open area with a wheel sticking up and the apparent driver had both hands on that. Brandon walked to the sporty looking thing and said, "Howdy."

The man driving whipped off his goggles and hat and said, "I'm sorry to have frightened your team, but the road isn't very smooth and causes a lot of noise from the metal buckling."

Brandon said, "My names Brandon Chedlow sir and I'm interested in this infernal machine of yours."

The driver said, "My name is Winchell Bruin, this lady in the back seat is my wife Jennie and beside me is my brother Hugh Bruin."

Brandon introduced Naundas to them and then asked them where they were bound and did he know there was a toll road not far ahead. Winchell exclaimed, "A toll road, well, I never thought it would come to that."

Brandon suggested he think about paying the toll, because the alternative wasn't a good choice. Brandon asked Winchell what he and his were doing up here in the hills and received a decent answer. Winchell stated he was looking for a person who made wonderful little expensive trinkets from different things. He wanted to make a deal with her to open a shop down in Charleston that sold only her creations. Brandon said, "Sounds like you're talking about my niece Shelly Willow."

Winchell become excited and said, "Well, yes I'm talking about Shelly Willow and of all things, I meet her uncle on the road and half scare his team to death. Well I'm prepared to offer her a 75/25% deal and she will make the lions share."

Brandon said, "You know what I think?" Winchell was all ears. Brandon continued with, "Twenty-five-seventy-five split is unfair, I think a sixty-forty split would be more on the level."

Winchell got a surprised look on his face and came back with, "Well you had better write a note to your niece explaining that to her sir."

Brandon said, "Before I do sir, there is one thing you must understand. If any advantage is taken of that widow, then I will come looking for you."

Then he assumed his gunfighters stance. Winchell took in the strapped down Forty-Four and shivered. He said, "Your point is well taken sir, but misplaced. I have no intentions of any skullduggery concerning your niece. I believe she and I will have a successful partnership."

Winchell let Brandon and Naundas take the team down the road before starting the noisy machine. Still when Winchell fired it up, the horses hit a dead run instantly. It took Brandon a half mile to bring them under control. Brandon told Naundas that maybe they would wait to buy one of those things, until the manufactures quieted them down a bit. They both got a good laugh at that.

CHAPTER TWENTY-FOUR

The baby had one set of lungs in its chest and let a yell go that froze Brandon's heart. He tickled the little boy under the chin and it stopped yelling and gurgled instead. Naundas was smiling at the two from her hospital bed in Charleston, West Virginia.

She had gotten pregnant just after the meeting of the Bruin Family and finally told Brandon while enjoying one of the most beautiful sunrises she had ever seen. The sun was blood red as it peeked up through the waters of the Atlantic Ocean. When it got through to Brandon that he was going to be a father, he just about woke up everything that might have been asleep within miles with a war whoop that sounded like a rebel yell to her. He immediately began trying to do everything for her until she put a stop to that with the words, "You will spoil me and make me fat, is that what you want my dear?"

"Well, hell, I'll just go and chop some wood then and leave you alone." He said it with a grin on his face.

Laying in the hospital bed she thought back over the last nine months since they left Shelly's house and knew they had done some good things. The shop Winchell built was right downtown Charleston and did a brisk trade. The best thing to come out of all that was the union of Shelly and Hugh Bruin. Hugh was an unmarried bachelor and fell hard for Shelly. The three children were his from hello and they were married at Christmas time. Brandon and Naundas hired a car to take them to the wedding. They surprised Shelly and they had a wonderful reunion. Shelly thanked Brandon for the letter of introduction to the Bruins and told him the business was doing well and she was thinking about starting a small factory here to make the artifacts faster. Brandon told her not to sacrifice quality for quantity. She said" "Good point, I'll think on it some more."

That was six months ago, now here she was a mother and more important than that, Brandon was a father and no prouder father existed on earth.

The little boy's name was Charles Dean Chedlow. Brandon had remembered his long dead friend Charley in a very special way and with the whole hearted consent of Naundas. She more than anyone, knew Brandon would never have had a real chance in life, if not for Charley taking him under his wing.

The child seemed to grow up so fast it scared Brandon. One day he was bouncing a baby on his knee and the next the child following him around wherever he went. The boy was naturally inquisitive and learned to converse with others before he reached two years old.

The Chedlows took up residence just off the beach near the port city of Chesapeake, Virginia. Brandon had sought a beach house that wasn't too elaborate and he wanted it to be homely as well. They drove their new Oldsmobile where ever they could, looking at many different houses. The one they chose struck both of them the moment it came in sight. Little Chuck as he was called become very animated at the sight of the house and the moment the Olds came to a halt he went faster than a bullet for the back yard. By the time Brandon and Naundas arrived the boy was swinging high in a swing tied to the limb of the only tree in sight. Brandon smiled and, "Well I sure hope we like the rest of this house because that boy has laid claim to the back yard."

Naundas laughed delightedly and said, "Let's go look honey"

They both went to the front door and used the key to open up. The house was low ceilinged and had beautiful leather furniture in the huge living room, hard wood floors and wall papered walls. There were huge windows affording a broad panoramic view of the beach. Brandon thought Naundas was going to swoon on him and he understood why. He said, "I would go back to gold mining again to own this. Let's buy it sweetheart."

Naundas said, "I'm with you hon."

That was two years ago and the three were completely happy living there. Brandon doted on his son and went everywhere with him. He joined a shooting club to keep current with his gun, but at forty-eight he reckoned his gunslinger days were behind him. That is until he came home one day and found Naundas chopped to death by unknown assailants.

He walked in and he and his son saw blood everywhere. The body of his beloved wife had been dragged all over the one story house, bleeding profusely, then killed in the kitchen. Brandon held his wife's lifeless body and carried it to their bedroom and laid her on their bed and covered her up. He felt sorry for his son Chuck, this was his first encounter with violence and the boy was in shock. Brandon took him in his arms and just held him. The boy plaintively said, "Mommy dead daddy."

Brandon didn't know what to say to his son, so he just held him and both cried their grief out for hours.

The sheriff came right away and was sickened by what someone had done. He reckoned it had to be smugglers. Brandon immediately went out on the beach and looked for footprints. He found none that entered his property and felt the perpetrators had come from town.

His wife was laid to rest on Sunday and it rained all day long matching his and Charles's tears. The saddest time was when they went home and there was no Naundas to greet them, both broke down and wept for hours.

One miserable day seemed to follow another. The memory of happiness was gone from their life and both were miserable. Brandon couldn't sleep in the main bed, so he slept with his son and both cried themselves to sleep each night. The Sheriff came around a couple of times, just to tell them no progress had been made in the case.

Brandon woke up on the twentieth day after the killing and become angry. He needed revenge. He had a four year old son to think of.

He woke Chuck and had him pack clean clothes and toys for a trip. He did the same, but his toy was a colt Forty-Four with extra ammo. He was going hunting by damn. If whoever did this thought they were getting away with it, they had another think coming. He and Chuck locked the house up and drove west towards the mountains.

The Oldsmobile seemed to work OK. for Brandon with the exception of scaring the daylights out of horses. He pulled into Shelly and Hugh's house at daylight on the second day. Chuck was sound asleep on the back seat. He had the top installed, so it had been a warm trip for the boy. When Brandon told Shelly about Naunda's death and the details Shelly began bawling like a baby. Her three children woke up and were crying as well. Brandon asked Shelly if she could handle Chuck for a spell while he looked for those that murdered his mother and she said, "For as long as it takes uncle, for as long as it takes."

CHAPTER TWENTY-FIVE

The trip back to the house was the loneliest trip Brandon had ever taken in his life and made him want to turn around and go back, grab his son and disappear into the mountains. Then he would get blinding mad and his resolve would reassert itself and he went on.

Back at the house he parked the Oldsmobile and went to town on the horse to visit the sheriff. He had his bedroll and Forty-Four and was ready for the chase. The sheriff had no news and Brandon left in a bit of a huff, because the man was just sitting on his fat ass and doing nothing. Brandon rode down the coast road and stopped to talk to everyone he met.

There were a fair amount of beach houses along the beach. Most were shut up for the season, but the ones where he did find people, the people did remember the killing and were now more prone to keep their doors locked than before. His one constant question was; had they seen anything unusual around the time his wife was murdered. Most give the question due consideration and answered with sincerity.

He went for days before he hit on a lead. He had ridden into a fish camp not many miles south of his house and the proprietor was an old Scotsman, that would talk one's leg off if given half a chance. His name was Buford and he had lived here for almost fifty years and seen a lot in those years. He welcomed Brandon's company and cooked enough seafood to feed a boy scout troop. Brandon ate his fill and told the nice old guy he was fuller than a boot. He finally got around to asking his standard question and got his first lead. He knew what he was chasing and what he was in for. Buford was quiet for some time before he spoke. He said, "There was something that bothered me about that time young man. It took me a long time to make up my mind to tell you about it, because what I saw could cost you your life, along with others."

Brandon was hanging on his every word. He said, "There were three men, Cubans or south Americans I think. They came in and asked me to prepare a seafood meal for them. They gave me the creeps, but business is business and I did as they requested. One in particular must have been the leader and wore a machete in a scabbard. The other two catered to this man and he had the look of a killer in his eyes."

Brandon turned cold all over because he knew his wife's killer was being described to him. Buford knew it too and felt sorry for his new friend. Brandon had him tell everything he could remember about the three and describe the boat to a tee they left in. Buford said, "It was a sail boat, something like thirty feet long and they anchored it out there in the bay and came in in a row boat. The boat was blue and white with gold lightning bolts painted on her bow."

Brandon asked, "Did you see her name sir?"

Buford said, "There was a name but my old eyes couldn't make it out except for the first letter and that was an M."

Brandon left the very next morning, after ascertaining the three murderers had sailed south. He stuck to the coast. Sometimes this was hard because some river would jump up that he had to cross. There were gators in these rivers and he feared for his horse's life at times, but was able to see the critters coming and used up a fair bit of Forty-Four ammo trying to shoot the ones who thought the two of them were food. The bugs were horrible and made him want to be elsewhere, but he wanted those three killers in the worst way and if it took putting up with a few blood sucking Mosquitoes, then so be it.

Brandon couldn't believe his eyes! There sitting in the bay was the boat described by old

Buford. Painted on her bow was "MEGOMETRY" and she looked deserted. There was no row boat on her deck either. Brandon's heart was beating in his throat and going a mile a minute. He had waited too long for this to mess it up now.

He went down to the water's edge until he found the row boat. There were three sets of prints leading from where the row boat was beached, inland and they were fairly fresh. He ran to his horse, mounted and begin tracking the three. The tracks led straight to a small group of houses just off a cove that the water looked very shallow in. He got down and staked his mount back in some scrub, grabbed some extra ammo and proceeded by foot to a trail that led to the houses.

He assumed a leisurely attitude, so as not to alert anyone, especially the killers. There seemed to be no one around as he entered the sandy street between the houses and then he heard a muffled scream from the second house and was instantly galvanized into action. He knew of no other way to do it, he just took the door off its hinges with a body slam and his gun ready to blaze away. What he saw made him see red and his gun to blaze away, a man with a machete was raping a woman who had blood all over her while his two sidekicks were looking on with pleasure written all over their faces.

Brandon shot the rapist in the left eye ball killing him instantly. Then he killed the other two with shots to their hearts. The raped woman was trying to cover herself up and Brandon took a look at her wounds and saw they were superficial and then he put a cover over her he found on the floor. She was incoherent and babbling words that didn't make sense to him.

He tried to talk to her and find if anyone else was hurt, but gave up and went looking for himself. He found the man of the house out back, with his severed head laying three foot from him. Both of these folks looked young and made Brandon look around for children, but he found none. Back inside he tried to attend to the girls wounds, but each time he touched her she began screaming and crawling away from him. Her worst wound was the one to her mind and only time could heal that.

Brandon buried her husband in a little graveyard along the trail out back. He went to each house, but found them all deserted and full of filth. The only house livable was the one that he had knocked the door down on. He went back to the girl and began to talk soothingly to her.

For the longest time she failed to respond and just stared at nothing. He got some water from a bucket in the kitchen and wet her lips. She drank greedily after that and then closed her eyes and went to sleep. Brandon sat for hours listening to her mutter in her sleep. She woke up hours later and looked at him and clear as day said, "Who are you and what are you doing in our house?"

Brandon told her who he was and she suddenly remembered and her world fell apart once more. He knew he had to get her in a bed, so he braved her fighting and lifted her to a bedroom off to the side he had noticed before. She kicked and screamed like a cat until she passed out. He took that opportunity to bandage her up a bit. He found sheets and ripped them into bandages for her wounds and finished just as she came around and started all over again Brandon said, "Look lady, I am a friend and I killed all three of those men that hurt you and if you let me, I want to help you."

The effect of his little speech was an amazing thing to see. She looked at him and asked, "Did you kill all three of them?"

Brandon smiled and said, "I did, because of what they were doing to you and what they did to my wife a month ago north of here"

The girl improved with each passing moment, but was set back somewhat when Brandon told her that her husband was dead. She got a quizzical look on her face and said, "I don't have a husband, that must be my brother you are talking about, the mean one took him outside while the other two raped me. I'm sorry he was killed."

Brandon asked, "How old are you my dear?"

She said, "I'm twenty-three and considered an old maid," then added, "I had never had a man before those three had their way with me."

Brandon had tears running down his cheeks because of the plaintive way she said it and tears were running down her face as well.

Brandon told the girl he was going hunting for some food for the two of them and her brown eyes followed him out the door he had re-hung.

He shot a deer not a mile from the houses and saw the boat still floating at anchor in the bay He knew he must go out there sometime, but he wasn't quite ready for that. He dressed the deer out and took the meat to the house. He found a reasonably clean kitchen to cook in and made a broth of the fat from around the little deer's neck.

He took a bowl of the soup to the girl and asked her her name. She said in a small voice with a Cajun lilt, "I'm Meleney, Reafly."

She took the bowl of meat and broth and ate it right down and asked for more. Brandon thought this girl has a strong constitution and will do alright. Brandon asked if she had any relatives around close and she said, "There are none I know of and before mom and dad passed on, they said the same thing."

That answered Brandon's next question and he grew quiet and said, "Well there is the sail boat that is anchored off shore."

Meleney shuddered and said, "Not in a million years would I step on that boat sir and I hope you don't ever make me."

CHAPTER TWENTY-SIX

Meleney improved daily and soon was up and around. She was a pretty thing and Brandon wondered why some man had never won her heart. She became inquisitive about him and asked all sort of questions. He told her all and she just set there with deer eyes taking it all in.

He buried the outlaws in a common shallow grave without fanfare, and stuck the machete in the ground as marker with one word on a board. It said "Murderers"

On the tenth day Brandon told her they should travel north unless she was game to stay here by herself. She shuddered and said, "I have nothing here and would like very much to go with you Brandon."

Brandon liked this girl and saw no reason to leave her behind to struggle alone. He liked her company and life didn't seem so lonely when she was around.

The two stood on the beach and watched the sail boat sink below the waves and disappear from sight. Brandon had taken the row boat and an ax out and holed her just below the water line and rowed back ashore. There were tears in Meleney's eyes as she went through a small bit of trauma seeing that boat, but she was happy to see it sank from sight.

CHAPTER TWENTY-SEVEN

Meleney had some real heart stopping nightmares over the next month and many times she woke up screaming and brought Brandon at a run to her bedroom. He found that the only way to calm her was to wrap her in his arms and hold her until it passed. This led to her depending on him to calm her and Brandon wasn't ready for a love relationship yet, because his wife wasn't long enough dead. He resisted the girl and knew it hurt her because she had fallen hard in love with him and he wanted at times to take her but found his wife's face floated before him each time. He left her crying but calm each time. He sat her down and explained all this to her and she said, "Brandon you just remember this, you will always be my knight in shining armor forever and I'll wait for you as long as it takes."

There were tears running down both of their cheeks by the time Brandon left the room.

Get your things together girl we are going to go get my son. Brandon had told Meleney all about his son and now Brandon felt it time to bring him home. They had been apart for a month and a half.

Meleney had never ridden in a car before and was reluctant to get in. Brandon finally convinced her it was safe and two mile down the road she was having the time of her life. The roads seemed to be improving some and mostly they cruised along at the mind numbing speed of twenty-two miles per hour. They arrived at Shellie's place mid-morning of their second day.

Chuck, just like he did each day had been waiting for the sight of the Oldsmobile and his dad. When it came in view he bolted for the door and was on the running board before Brandon was able to stop. He wrapped his arms around his father and then noticed Meleney and become shy. Brandon introduced the girl and Chuck and they looked at each other and Chuck figured if she was someone his father sanctioned that was alright with him, so he politely said, "Hello Meleney."

She said, "Hello Chuck, pleased to meet you."

The boy turned his attention to his father and asked, "Will we be going home dad?"

Brandon laughed and said, "Well, you can bet on that son."

The real hard part was telling his son he had killed the three that killed his mother. The boy had tears in his eyes and bowed his head then looked at his father and said, "Good Dad, they were mean men,"

After he told his boy about how he had met Meleney, the boy got up and went to her and hugged her with tears in his eyes. The two bonded after that and become inseparable.

CHAPTER TWENTY-EIGHT

There was not a thing to be done about it. The day had started out normal with Chuck going off to school down the road and Brandon sitting at the dining table drinking his coffee and reading the financial times. He heard a noise in the bedroom where Meleney slept and went to investigate and found her standing in the center of the room in a state of undress. She had the most exquisite body with the most provocative breast and the biggest eyes and all this brought desire to him in waves and he knew it would be fine with Naundas if this union took place. He rushed to her and enveloped her in his arms. They both fell to her bed and made love like they had been doing it for ever.

The couple, coupled many times that day and knew they were in love and it felt right. When Chuck came home from school he looked from one to the other and his face grew red. He wasn't overly upset, but he needed to be told what had taken place in his absence. They all sat down and Brandon explained. "Son when your mother was killed by those evil men it devastated me and almost destroyed me too. When I found the man doing the same thing with Meleney, I killed them and rescued her from the same fate that your mother suffered. Now your mother is gone, but don't you think she might want this wonderful person here looking after you and me in her absence?"

Chuck was silent for a minute and then he looked at them both and said, "I think maybe you're right Dad and I do like Meleney, it's OK with me."

He smiled at them both and all three laughed.

Brandon was on his knee proposing to Meleney and Chuck was urging her on saying, "Say yes Meleney, say yes!"

It was now May, and they were in the living room of their house on the beach. The two had gotten along wonderful over the wintertime and were as one.

The towns folk had lifted a brow or two at the difference in their ages, and in the 1900's this was of some concern to the righteous of the community. They had gotten a posse together to make their discontent known to the unwed couple. The good town's people had marched to

Brandon's front door and presented themselves. As luck would have it, Brandon wasn't in a real great mood. Seems some wild stock broke his fence down to get at his tame stock and he had just spent a good three hours repairing wire and removing two wild mustangs from his property.

When he heard the knock on the door he went to answer it and was faced with some irate town folk that demanded he not live in sin with a woman half his age. He leveled a long look at the pompous bunch and said, "OK I'll ask her to be my wife today and your church can marry us. Is that satisfactory to you?"

The mob deflated and had no comeback for that. They had expected a battle and now were chastened into silence and left. Brandon was still laughing when Meleney came in the room from in the back. She wanted to know what was funny and all Brandon said was, "The town folk that's all."

Meleney looked at him strangely but didn't press it. That was one of the reasons they got along so well. If Brandon wanted her to know something he always told her at the optimum time. Brandon had waited until his son came home from school and then had sprang the news that it was time for the wedding.

The wedding took place on the following Saturday afternoon and more people showed up than he expected and made for a gala affair. The reception was held at the beach Hotel Grand House and cost Brandon a mint , but he thought it was worth it. Meleney was a beautiful bride and caused him to think of how close she had come to being a dead body like her brother had. She was dear to him and he would fiercely protect her for as long as he had breath left in his body. Meleney knew there would never be another man for her and had given her heart completely to Brandon the moment she had become coherent after being raped. She now realized this man had saved her life in more ways than she could count.

CHAPTER TWENTY-NINE

The ship was a colossal mess as far as Brandon was concerned and he would be happy to get himself and family off the thing. They were approaching Sydney Bay on the good ship Starstorm, with a registry in Amsterdam and was on the verge of being replaced with steam powered metal hull passenger ships.

This was the only method of getting to Australia short of buying a sea going sailing yacht and becoming his own captain. He had given just that some serious thought, but his wife Meleney and his son Chuck both nixed the idea and convinced him that would be a stupid thing to do. He instead approached the shipping company and bought three tickets to Sydney, Australia. The crossing had been a nightmare for the three. The trip around the horn had pretty much convinced Brandon that he would never set foot on another sail boat, if he ever got off this damn one that is. Once they rounded the corner and sailed north along South America, the boat leveled off and the three could walk about without climbing a hill or going down one each time they walked on deck.

Sydney was a city of almost a million people and about half of them were prisoners sent by the British Rulers to establish a penal colony in order to empty out their prisons. Seems if you failed to pay any debt in that country, you could get a free trip to this new colony. The only thing was that, if one kept himself out of trouble he could become a free man in seven years. There were more women than there should be, because they came to Australia on their own behest, only to find most of the men in servitude of some sort.

The only reason Brandon came to this arid desert was he had heard about a gold find called Lassiter's reef. It was purported to be solid gold. An old miner had carried a chunk of the stuff out that weighed somewhere near a hundred pounds. The old fellow died before he could get back to the reef and its where bouts went to the grave with him. Different prospectors had searched for the reef, but to no avail. The desert was harsh and many didn't prepare well and perished from their lack of understanding of that desert.

Brandon thought he had enough experience to survive in that desert and felt he had an even chance of finding Lassiter's reef.

Brandon figured that gas mobiles weren't reliable enough to go into the desert with and elected to go with a wagon that he designed himself. He had heard horror stories of the sand being so deep and the temperature so hot that horses and men fell dead from over exertion. He wanted to make it easy to travel over soft sand. The iron wheels he had made by a blacksmith were a foot wide and as sturdy as possible.

The blacksmith was from the old country and took a shine to Brandon and his wife and son. Chuck was growing like a weed and was now taller than his step mother. He helped his dad and the blacksmith build their wagon while Meleney sat watching them. Brandon took the three of them to lunch in one of the many eating houses that afforded most any cuisine imaginable. They all had seafood and it was second to none because it was caught and cooked all in the same day. The cost was so little that Brandon was sure a mistake had been made, and since he couldn't understand the waiter, he just let it ride.

Brandon wanted special water containers. He settled for whisky barrels, that his blacksmith put double bands around. There were four of these and were mounted on the side of the wagon. These four barrels would be the bulk of the weight on the wagon. There would be bedding and cooking utensils and food. There was no feed for the horses out there he was told, so they carried grain along for them as well.

When the outfit was all together it was impressive. There were two saddle horses with western saddles they had brought from home. The two team horses were small horses compared to the saddle ones, but folks assured them those two little horses would in fact pull a great load and not eat him out of grain at the same time.

CHAPTER THIRTY

The shake down run was ran on the softest sand they could find down near the beach and the little horses had no problem pulling the big wide tired wagon through it. They only needed food stuff. aboard now in order to be on their way and went about town buying this and that at many different stores. They were told that Kangaroo was a delicious meat and there were millions of the pests all over the place.

It was like they had fallen off the earth the first hour they traveled north away from Sydney. There was a well-defined track that had some traffic on it. Most were lines of prisoners being moved where ever. Meleney felt sorry for some of them because they were being herded in chains like they were cattle. Brandon told her they shouldn't meddle in the affairs of the English guards. Meleney said, "As long as they left them alone, she would leave them alone."

She said it in such a way that both Chuck and Brandon become tickled at her.

Camp that first night was on a creek that had a small spring fed Billy Bong with lily pads and frogs making their funny rivet sound. They had been warned of the possibility of deadly snakes and possible Crocodile taking residence in the waters both with humans on their list of edible food. There was fish in Billy Bongs as well and Chuck had while growing up on America's east coast become an avid fisherman and proceeded to supply them with Barramundi that cooked up like an American Rainbow Trout did. There were some hungry fish in that Billy Bong and Chuck kept his parents busy filleting and drying and smoking the delicious meat.

They stayed there for three days and had a good supply of both dried fish and Roo meat. As far as Brandon could tell the Kangaroo should have evolved into a deer. The head was like a deer and the meat matched deer meat in taste and texture. They were easier to kill however and one day he shot one and after it was down, a little Joey popped his head out of her pouch. Brandon really felt bad then and without meaning to they become surrogate parents to the little kangaroo. Brandon had extracted the little fellow from his mother's pouch and it hopped around as he butchered its mother and made him so sad that he picked it up and put it in the wagon. The little Joey hung its head out and looked everywhere. Meleney fed the little tyke powdered milk mixed with water and it seemed to satisfy the orphan completely. Chuck named him Orvel and he would come when they spoke to him. Orvel was a grand pet. He didn't make any messes and sat on his tail around camp and loved his ears scratched. Chuck and Orvel took to traveling together. Chuck would lead on his horse and Orvel was right there and could move faster than a horse could. Orvel was a good edition to the safari and kept them entertained with his antics.

When the blue inland mountains were leveling out to plains, Brandon turned west. There were no tracks to follow so he took compass readings often. The terrain was semi-arid and water become scarce. They filled up the barrels each time they came to water, if it was sweet to drink. Towns were few and were usually next to a ranch, called a station over there. The stations either ran cattle or sheep, but rarely both.

There were Aboriginals all along the way, who would stand in silence and watch them pass, some would come out and try trading different things such as boomerangs that were made out of some of the heaviest wood Brandon had ever seen. He traded some dried fish for one and gave it to Chuck. Chuck began throwing the thing, but it wouldn't come back and animals had nothing to fear from him what-so-ever.

One day an Aboriginal came from nowhere and stood there until Chuck noticed the mostly undressed boy. The native took the boomerang and sailed it through the air and it made a complete circle and landed not three feet in front of them. Chuck made an attempt to copy after him and the thing did turn the corner but fell to the ground. The native grunted and motioned that he needed to throw harder. Chuck was a pretty strong young man now and he really put some power into the throw the next time and they both had to get out of the way quick because the damn thing tried to decapitate the both of them. The Aboriginal grabbed Chuck and they both went down laughing. The boomerang bounced on some rocks behind them.

The boy's name was Ulay as near as they could figure. He stayed around them for days and taught Brandon and Meleney where to find water when there seemed to be none. He cut some bamboo at a Billy bong and with great skill used a smaller stick to hollow it out making it into a tube. With this tube he went into the first dry creek bed they came to and worked it down into the sand a good three feet. He began sucking on the bamboo and soon spit out sand and water;

each time he did this he capped the tube with his thumb keeping the prime of his make do well.

Ulay showed Chuck how the boomerang was used as a hunting weapon. He killed a big bird no one knew the name of but the breast was delicious. The Aboriginal boy ate with them with his fingers and indicated his thanks and that he must go back to his tribe. They had gotten used to his company, but he must do what he must do. The only thing that hurt the three was their kangaroo went with the Aboriginal boy. The last time they saw Orvel, he was jumping high above the boys head and having a great time. Brandon heard that the natives didn't eat the Roo's and maybe that swayed ole Orvel over to Ulay.

Brandon was dozing in the front seat of the wagon and was brought rudely awake by the little team of horses trying to climb back towards the rear of their tongue that separated the two. He looked out front and saw two nightmares descending on him. Two of the wildest looking birds standing taller than a man with stubby wings flapping were laying siege on his wagon. Meleney and Chuck had their hands full just sticking in their saddles of their wildly bucking, snorting and squealing mounts. All Brandon knew to do was shoot the damn things. He whipped out his forty-four and did just that. He shot each one in the head from about twenty feet. Their momentum carried them almost to the team and the two little horses raised all Billy hell and tried to get away from the evil smelling things. Brandon jumped down and ran to their heads and calmed them down then turned them away from the dead birds.

Chuck and Meleney came riding up then and Chuck asked, "Dad, what are those things anyhow?"

Brandon said, "Well they're dead Emus that's what and I've heard they are good to eat, so start plucking family."

The meat was some of the reddest, fine grained meat they had seen and when broiled over an open fire was delicious to eat. They preserved the meat in much the same way beef was. They dried the stuff in the hot dry climate after salting it down.

The weather seemed to get hotter the farther they progressed into the interior of the great Simpson desert. Their destination was Lake Ayer in the dead center of the Flinders range. The lake was rumored to be a sometime thing and depended on the amount of rainfall, whether it was dry hole or lake.

The terrain become constant ridge after ridge and made making a lot of time impossible. Brandon inspected any exposed ridge for sign of gold. He noticed there were small seashells imbedded in the sand and gravel. That told him this at one time had been under the ocean and therefore could be classified as a reef and one of these out here was Lassitors. He inspected each thoroughly for any sign of gold and was rewarded with some nuggets in some sand one day. He backed off and looked at the reef and his heart began to beat harder. That gold must come from a source somewhere. He told Meleney and Chuck he thought maybe they should set up camp here and really do some serious prospecting.

CHAPTER THIRTY-ONE

It was so hot during the day the three hid from the sun and did their digging after it went down. There was a big moon hanging around and it sometimes got downright cold late at night. There was enough water, but it was used sparingly and Brandon made up his mind that when half of their water was gone they were returning to the coast no matter if they found gold or not.

It was hard digging in the dark and one night Brandon's shovel hit something that didn't sound like a rock. He wrestled the whatever it was aside and went on digging. They grew tired and decided to go to bed. The moon was setting and it would be pitch black before long. Brandon was so tired he slept like the dead. He was startled awake by his son Chuck shaking him and saying, "Dad come look, come look."

Brandon staggered out from his bed under the wagon and rubbed his eyes. Chuck led him out to the dig and down to the hole. Brandon saw what was exciting his son. There was the biggest gold nugget he had ever seen glinting in the sunlight. That was what he had pushed aside last night in the dark. They may not have found Lassitors Reef, but they dang sure had found Chedlow Reef.

That day, before it got too hot, the three took more gold out of that reef than they could haul back to the coast. Brandon had taken compass readings all the way to this reef and felt confident he could find it again. Just to make sure he and Chuck built a marker on the top of the reef. They loaded what Brandon thought would be a safe load and buried the rest below that rock marker.

The return trip was slower by a mile as the little horses had to struggle with the loaded wagon. In hard places Brandon and Chuck roped the wagon and let four horses pull the thing, this worked well. The animals had to have water and the barrels were dangerously low by the time they hit Broken hill.

It was no more than a cattle station with a store and water bore. A windmill pumped water into what was called a turkey nest, but was nothing more than an earth dike that held water where all things watered. Brandon filled the barrels from a pipe coming straight from the windmill and it was steaming hot. He bought two additional horses and harness. The little horses needed a rest. He met the station owner and found him a nice fellow. They were invited out to Jum wah station for a spell, to catch their breath, the owner Neil Bottoms said. Brandon was happy to go out and visit because they did need a break from thirty-five days on the trail. Neil commented that the wagon looked pretty heavy and Brandon said, "Well its got quite a load on it."

Neil raised an eyebrow, but said no more.

Jum-wah station resembled a well kept ranch and impressed the Chedlow's greatly. Mrs. Bottoms was a gracious hostess and made them feel welcome. They were led to clean cool rooms and told where a bath could be had. The hands about the Station would help them in anyway. She said hot water is being prepared as we speak and a laundry will take your dirty clothes and make them clean for you. Brandon couldn't help think boy, there should be more places like this one out here. Bathed and with clean clothes on, made them feel like a million bucks.

Neil their host, welcomed them to a large living room with leather furniture and warm wood tones on the walls. He said, "I have a guard on your wagon sir and if you need, there is a safe of gigantic proportions right over there."

Brandon laughed and said, "Thank you sir, but I think that would be an awful amount of work transferring my gold in here. There's not a piece under a hundred pounds in the lot."

Neil's eyes grew big and he said quietly, "You found Lassitors reef didn't you sir?"

Brandon said, "I don't know if I did or not sir, but there's a bunch of gold still there, but I don't think I want to go back for it. I'm already a rich man and I'm getting along in years and don't need the money anymore. Maybe someday my son may want to go back there and if he does, the way is mapped for him."

CHAPTER THIRTY-TWO

The ship they chose to go back home was such a beauty that took their breath away. It was a far cry from the wooden one they had come to Sydney in. She was named STAR and was the first steam ocean going ship to enter Sydney Harbor. There were lots of reporters in the crowd and some photographer was taking flashing photos of the new ship. Brandon had only just made the list of passengers. The thing was booked solid and he only got three tickets because someone had cancelled. Their gold and goods had been loaded and they were only waiting to board.

Meleney was excited beyond any previous times she could remember. They were going to make history by being on the first steam ship to travel the pacific ocean and would head east. The star had her keel laid in Melbourne, Australia. There were other steam ships on the waters of the world, but the Aussies were rightly proud of building this one.

Once aboard they were totally impressed by the posh interior of the ship. Brandon couldn't believe the difference in comfort compared to the sail ship that made them wish for dry land from the first day aboard. This thing was like a floating grand hotel. Chuck ran all over the ship causing the ships personnel to smile. Their cabin was simply beautiful. There were port holes to open and their view was of the ocean and one lower deck. They had never seen flush toilets before and were suitably impressed with the things.

The STAR docked in San-Francisco without incident after a seven week crossing of the pacific ocean. The Chedlow's had to learn to walk again on dry land and leave their sea legs behind. Meleney was the funniest of all. She had to hang on to Brandon to stay on her feet until she gained her equilibrium once again.

The gold was taken to the San-Francisco gold exchange and caused quite a stir with the assayer. He wanted to know where this gold came from and Brandon said with a grin, "Well, you go west for seven weeks on a boat, then continue west for thirty days overland and if you are very lucky you might find where it came from."

The train trip through the rocky mountains was a slow ride, but afforded the three some spectacular views of breath taking shear mountain sides where the railway had been built. Meleney hid her face in Brandon's arm pit and wouldn't look out until Brandon assured her the train was back where there were two sides of land. Chuck was having a wonderful time and went from car to car looking out windows.

They arrived in Charleston West Virginia after fourteen days and nights on a train that had its water and coal replenished many times all across the country. They hired a car to take them on to Virginia and home to the coast. The house was still intact and in good order through out. The Oldsmobile fired right up and that amazed Brandon all to hell. The three were happy to be home and Meleney took to cleaning and ran the two men out of the house. They went fishing and brought enough red snapper home, to feed the lot of them for a week.

Brandon was approaching fifty-eight years old and starting to feel it. He noticed he had tingling fingers on his left hand and secretly sought out a doctor about it. The doctor told him what he already suspected. His heart was failing on him and about the only thing he could do for him was give him some nitro pills for pain and he should take it easy and be sure to get plenty of rest.

Brandon held his hand up and bluntly asked, "How long do I have doc?"

The doctor's face grew red and he threw his hands up then said, "Mr. Chedlow, get your things in order, because you may not last the month out."

Brandon thought, there now we know don't we. He went from the doctor's office to his lawyer's and put everything in order. He made a will that gave all his holdings equally to Meleney and his son. He went home and called a meeting and told his loved ones his story. Chuck and Meleney were in tears by the time he was through. He did tell them he would last as long as he could and wasn't going to stop living before he stopped breathing. The three were in each other's arms then.

Brandon got up from bed and went to the newly installed flush toilet and sat on it, he was in the middle of his daily constitutional when he felt something give way in his chest and a great pain enveloped him and he died still sitting on his toilet. Meleney found him there thirty minutes later. She screamed and Chuck came at a run.

Brandon was laid to rest on his own property, near the trail leading to their beach. There were more than a hundred people there to say goodbye. The gunslinger had ran out of time.

Part II
Son of a Gunslinger

CHAPTER THIRTY-THREE

Charles Dean Chedlow was devastated by his father's death and grieved mightily over it. He was only fifteen when his father died of heart failure and was sixteen before he got over it enough to put his life back in order. His stepmother, Meleney, grieved right along with him. The two came out of their grief good friends. Meleney worshipped her stepson and made his life as easy as it could be. Charles wanted some education and pursued that goal. He finished High school with flying colors and enrolled at the Virginia school for higher learning near their home.

Charles secretly had practiced with guns and could shoot better than most folks could by the time he was eighteen. Charles figured the day of gun fighters had passed, still he learned to draw and hit a target and thought he was pretty fast, but there was no one to test himself against. He drew on his horse and the horse blinked her eyes each time he drew fast and become agitated at him. Charles had to assure his horse he wasn't going to shoot her and the horse named, Filly, nuzzled him and nickered.

Meleney watched her stepson develop into a mountain of a man. He was six foot six and had to bend down below the door sill to enter the house. There were Plenty of girls after the man he had become and Meleney tried to run interference for him and keep the boy from loosing his head over some little hotty. As far as Charles was concerned, some little hotty was just what he needed to settle down his hormones to a livable stage.

Meleney was as a devoted mother as she could be and wanted no other man in her life other than Charles. She made sure he was clothed and she taught him manners so he wouldn't fall on his face at any function. The young man was fast becoming a voice people listened too. He gave several speeches at his school on the subject of how to live one's life in a manner that benefited society as a whole and not just the person. He established a trust fund with some of the money he helped to extract from mother earth. This trust fund would be for scholarships for higher learning for financially challenged youngsters that excelled in the first twelve years of their education. He named the fund the Brandon fund and it grew by leaps and bounds and soon had to be managed by people trained in such matters. Charles was fast becoming recognizable at any function about campus and there was almost always a pretty lady on his arm.

CHAPTER THIRTY-FOUR

"You're going to do what?" Meleney was facing off her stepson and was somewhat perturbed at him.

He had just told her he was going into the US Army with the rank of Second Lieutenant, when he graduated university in three months. Meleney went from crying over her loss, to feeling so proud she preened and when he came home in his smart tailored sand and olive drab uniform she had the proudest moment of her life.

The war in Europe was heating up and the French were calling for American volunteer's to fill their ranks. They had made a terrible misjudgment when the Maginot defense line at her north east border with Germany was built in anticipation that the Germans would attempt to conquer France. Great gun placements had been constructed to repel the Huns when they attacked Mother France. The guns were a marvel, however the guns couldn't be reversed to fire the other way and this was responsible for the deaths of millions of Frenchmen. The Germans overran the gun placements and the French were forced to fight a much superior force without any artillery whatsoever; because the guns couldn't be turned around. Once the battle was carried to the rear of the guns the Germans slaughtered French soldiers by the hundreds of thousands.

This is what had Meleney shaking inside, because her son had volunteered as an advisor to the French forces. As an officer, he would be behind the lines, but still be subject to artillery barrages. Charles did his best to convince his stepmother there wasn't much danger in what he would do over there and he would return shortly.

CHAPTER THIRTY-FIVE

This wasn't supposed to be how it worked. Charles was hunkered down in a trench up to his ass in mud, while artillery shells landed all around and if one happened to land in the trench with him he would be vaporized and never missed. The Head Quarters had come under attack before dawn and even the colonel was stuck in this mud hole.

Charles as an artillery officer, couldn't believe the French had no artillery piece's to return fire with. He didn't know what to do. He had advised the colonel to come up with some big guns to take the battle to the enemy, instead the French forces were being decimated on an hourly basis. The colonel in typical French fashion, shrugged his soldiers and said, "There is none mon Lieutenant."

Charles made up his mind that when this siege let up, he was going to do what he should have done when he first arrived. He was going to get his ass out of here and go find some guns bring them back and pound the shit out of some Germans.

The French General in Paris was sympathetic, but couldn't help him. There simply were no guns in France. Charles kept right on going and a week later found himself in front of the English Vice Marshal for European operations in London. He was told the English were not yet involved in the war, but it wasn't all that far across the channel and if there was a danger of Jerry threatening the British empire then something must be done. Here he had firsthand intelligence from an American officer no less, that Jerry in fact had every intention of advancing right across the channel and conquering Mother England along with the rest of Europe.

The Vice Admiral wanted this officer to talk to others in his country and made sure he would have the best accommodation available.

Charles walked out of the Vice Marshal's office on air. He had gotten through to the Vice Marshal that the guns should be moved quickly before the Germans got wind of it and took action to stop them.

Charles was whisked to a beautiful hotel by car with a young girl as the driver. He fell in bed and was roused out by the same girl at seven AM and handed a dispatch from the Vice

Admiral. The girl said, "Read this and then come along with me. I'll be down stairs, and sir, fifteen minutes should be adequate for you to dress."

Charles ripped the dispatch open and the words jumped out at him. They were "Lieutenant, My boss wants a word with you."

Charles thought, now who would be the boss of the Vice Admiral of defense. Then it hit him, he was about to meet the Prime Minister of England. His hands shook as he folded the dispatch and pocketed it.

Charles was dressed and down stairs in a matter of three minutes after reading the note. The girl was setting in her car and when she saw him coming, she jumped out and opened the rear door for him. Twenty minutes later the car stopped on Downing Street and the girl jumped out and opened his door and with a smile said, "Have fun sir."

There was a stiff upper lipped butler sort of a man at the door and Charles said. "Lieutenant Chedlow, sir."

The stiff shirt said, "Welcome sir to the Prime Minister's home and office."

The Prime Minister was a short round man with an unlit cigar in his mouth. He appraised Charles with a level intelligent look, then said, "Welcome to my country lieutenant, please sit down."

The desk between them was at least ten foot square. The minister said, "You have put quite a scare into my Vice Admiral young man. How bad is it with the war in France?"

Charles was slow to answer because he knew these next few minutes could make or break him. He finally said, "There are no artillery pieces to fight the Germans with sir. The French have none and without them the French have nothing to stop the advance of the Huns. Their next stop is Paris and then on to the channel and across to here."

By the time Charles was finished, the Prime minister's was white and was visibly shaken. He wanted to know how many guns it would take to do the job and Charles said, "Even one gun would be better than we have now sir, but we need a battalion of Artillery at least to drive the Germans back out of France."

The Prime Minster said, "You will have your guns. They will be barged to Calais and then go by train to the front. You will be appointed as commander of the Battalion and we will send one man for each gun to train others."

Charles was silent for a moment and then asked the minister if it was proper that he, a second lieutenant, should command a battalion. The Prime Minister in the first show of human emotion laughed uproariously. He said, "I will call my counterpart in France and you will be an honorary colonel in the French army."

Charles took his leave of the Prime Minister of England and went to his hotel room and slept for eighteen hours straight.

A special train was formed in Calais, France and completely filled with wheeled artillery pieces and ammo. All Charles had to do now was make sure the men that came with the ordinance trained French gunners to shoot the damn things.

Back Paris the commanding French general. was much impressed with this brash young Second Lieutenant from America and as he was instructed from his boss, appointed him an honorary colonel in the French army. Charles simply went about his business of recruiting an artillery battalion. He found out right away this was easier then he first thought, simply because there were a multitude of men that was more than ready to get out of the trenches to the relative safety in the rear where artillery operated.

The first salvo of artillery had a dramatic effect on the Germans. After having no return fire for months, suddenly they were getting pounded daily and receiving casualties. It suddenly become unpopular to be stationed at the German front.

Charles was kept busy with the logistics of keeping his battalion supplied with everything from food, to ammo for the guns. He also had to train his commanders well and if they stayed in one place for more than one day, they stood the chance of the Germans zeroing on their position. They were taught to shoot and move and then do it again. After all wasn't that the reason wheels were installed on their guns?

Charles was called in front of the Commanding General in Paris and awarded the French legion of merit. This was one of the highest awards an American could receive and still be walking around. Charles couldn't understand why he was singled out for an award when he witnessed acts of heroism each day at the front.

The Germans had enough and with the bristling English joining the war effort decided that they should strategically withdraw beyond the Maginot line. They destroyed the guns as they fled and soon the war was being carried to the Germans in Germany.

Charles was getting tired and his colonel saw this and ordered him to Paris for a R and R. Charles turned his command over to a French colonel and went to Paris. He was put up in an exquisite little hotel not a stone's throw from the Seine River and spent his first night mostly in the bath tub, getting the grime off his body. He slept for two days and then went out to enjoy the pleasures only Paris in the 1900's could offer a soldier.

Charles was sitting at an outdoor café, when suddenly a beautiful girl was standing in front of him. She said something to him in French, but Charles held out his hands in a sign that he didn't understand. The girl smiled and ask in perfect English, if she could join him. Charles stood and said, "Oh! please do miss."

The girl was the most beautiful creature he had seen in this country and was expensively dressed in clothing that had to come from some exclusive shop somewhere. Charles was tongue tied. The girl took pity on him and said, "My name is Roshell, what's yours?"

He finally stammered, "Charles". She took his hand and he didn't want to ever let go. She finally withdrew her hand and said, "If you don't mind, I could sure use a coffee, that is if you will have one with me."

Right then Charles would have drank a gallon of anything, if it was her desire.

Roshell was easy to talk to and the two spent the better part of the day right there. Lunch was taken, but Charles couldn't remember what they had eaten. She told him her life story. She was a product of an American Father and a

French mother. Her father had died on a ship that went down a few years ago and her mother still lived here in Paris, sometime she would like him to meet her. Charles told his story and Roshell listened with huge eyes and exclaimed with ohs and ahs when she heard that he was the son of a gunslinger from the old west.

The day was all but spent when Roshell exclaimed that she must go and would he meet her right here at ten am for coffee tomorrow.

At nine, Charles was on station at the Café', at ten there was no sign of Roshell, but Charles had learned that French people were notorious for being late for everything. By twelve his heart was heavy and he got up and wondered down the walkway beside the river. He was sad and had made up his mind to return to his battalion today. He was about to turn on the cobble stone street leading to his hotel when he heard his name frantically being called.

He turned around and saw Roshell running towards him, yelling, "Charles, Charles." He moved towards her and the two fell into each other's arms and both knew things would never be the same again for either one of them. Roshell was crying and trying to explain what happened. She had been so excited about meeting him that she couldn't go to sleep until it was daybreak and had slept like the dead and not woke until afternoon. She was so very sorry and would never do that again. Charles steered her straight to his hotel and took her upstairs and consummated the relationship right then. The couple spent the full day in bed and only got up when hunger pains forced them to.

CHAPTER THIRTY-SIX

Charles went back to the front with a feeling of, "let's get this over with", because he had a reason not to be here now. He juiced his Company commanders up to a fever pitch of activity and demanded more targets from the forward echelon of command. His enthusiasm was infectious and more patrols were sent out and more targets were filtered down, The ammo from England was rushed up and trains were coming at a tremendous pace. The Germans were attempting to bomb the trains coming from Calais, but with the extreme short range and slow flight of the aircraft, it was almost a suicide mission to try. Because the train was heavily guarded along its path, not one shipment was lost.

Roshell pined away for him and waited patiently for his return. Her job in a department store didn't hold the same allure as before and she knew when her soldier came for her, she would give herself to him whole heartedly and go wherever he wanted her to.

Charles heard the shell coming and knew it had his name on it. He dove for the floor and rolled under his desk. The shell exploded not ten yards from him and the concussion knocked him into unconsciousness. His last thought was Roshell and things went black.

This was strange indeed, he was on his back in a bed and there was ropes attached to his bound body in different places. He hurt all over and could only move fingers and toes so he knew he wasn't paralyzed. His eyes could move back and forth but not his head. The cast was solid and made him realize he was probably broken up pretty bad inside. He remembered the shell and diving under his desk. He reckoned that this had probably saved his life.

A nurse finally looked in his eyes and exclaimed something in French he didn't understand then said in English, "Welcome back to the living lieutenant, you've had a rough time and will have some pain, but some morphine will help that."

She gave him a shot in an exposed area near his right elbow. A wonderful feeling came over him and he thought boy that's good stuff. He went right to sleep and only woke up when he smelled food. A different nurse younger than the first came in with a tray and spoon fed him. He asked her how long he had been here and she said, "Eight days now and you must be hungry sir and you can have all you want."

He realized these nurses were American and asked the young nurse about that. She replied with, "You are in a French Hospital in Paris, France, there are mostly American staff here. The war has turned around and Germanys surrender is eminent, since the allies have beaten them all the way back to the Rhine River."

Charles was ecstatic at the news and moved something that shouldn't be moved and the pain hit him in waves and he couldn't help the cry of pain that escaped from his lips. A doctor and another nurse were summoned and a huge shot of morphine administered. The pain was still with him when he went out.

Charles came back to consciousness by degrees. He thought there was someone sitting by his side, but he couldn't be sure. He woke with a feeling of being suffocated and tried to fight whoever was suffocating him off. Then he realized there were two warm lips on his and they felt wonderful. His eyes popped open and he saw Roshell's face before his. If he could have, he would have grabbed her and hung on for life, but he couldn't move a muscle without a great deal of pain coursing through his broken body. He said through gritting teeth, "I'm so sorry my darling, but I'm fairly beat up inside, and can't move anything without pain. How did you find me sweet Roshell?"

Roshell said, "My roommate is a nurse and she was telling me about this broken soldier they had brought off the battle field and all at once I had a feeling it was you she was talking about. I almost went wild making sure and in getting here. The doctor said you will probably make it ok, because there wasn't any bleeding. You had almost every bone in your body broken and those that weren't were badly bruised."

Charles began healing with the expert care he received from a caring hospital staff. Within days he was itching all over under his cast and hoped the damn thing could be removed soon before the itch drove him absolutely mad. His hands seemed less injured than the rest of his body did. The doctor came and said, We can remove the arm cast I think so you can eat without help. You must expect some pain and if it becomes severe I'll order a new cast installed.

Charles felt naked with his arm casts removed, but it was wonderful just to be able to scratch his itch. He had some difficulty reaching all the itch spots and enlisted Roshell to do them. This was some kind of funny and both felt ridiculous. He was black and blue from the bombs concussion and looked like a tattooed wild man. He was however healing up slowly.

CHAPTER THIRTY-SEVEN

The ship was festooned with more American flags than Meleney thought was possible. She was waiting for the offloading of troops returning from the war. Somewhere in that teaming mass was her stepson, Charles. She had worried herself half sick thinking she may never see him again and now here he was according to the telegram. She didn't quite understand why the message read, we are homeward bound, but she was too excited about his return to worry.

There he was and she was shocked to see that he was as thin as a rail. His uniform hung on him loosely and he looked gaunt. Her heart near broke as he made his way painfully down the ramp to where she waited. There was a beautiful young woman holding on to him and Meleney thought she must be his nurse. Charles saw his stepmother and said something to the girl and the two moved over to where she was. Charles went into his stepmother's arms. Meleney hung on to him and cried out her happiness. The nurse stood by and when the two broke apart Meleney said, "Oh, thank you nurse for bringing my son home to me."

Charles laughed when he noticed Roshell's red face. He said, "Meleney this is my wife Roshell. We were married ten days ago because that was the only way Roshell could travel with me. We wanted to wait till we got home, but that was not possible. There are no commercial ships running across the Atlantic and Roshell would have had to wait for one to come over otherwise." Meleney simply walked to Roshell and took her in her arms. She said, "Thank you for being there for my son Roshell and bringing him safely home to me."

CHAPTER THIRTY-EIGHT

Charles looked across the heaving seas at the white caps and thought this would be wild in a smaller boat. He was at the helm relieving the watch because he was the officer of the deck and the seaman first class had to have a toilet break. The two hundred foot Destroyer was easy to steer and he was able to stay the course of 220 degrees without difficulty. He knew the seaman would take at least the full fifteen minutes he was entitled to and drifted off into thoughts of the past.

Charles thought over the last three years of his life. He had taken him some time to heal up from his wounds and did it by being constantly near Roshell. She proved to be a jewel of a person and fit right into the big low house. His stepmother considered her to be a daughter and the two of them could laugh at almost anything together. When Charles mended to a point he could jog the beach trail, he and Roshell took to riding and this helped him to heal completely.

He separated from the Army with the rank of Captain. He had been promoted to first lieutenant by the US Army based on his honorary French promotion to Colonel then to Captain while flat on his back in the Paris Hospital with a cast covering his entire body.

Charles loved the sea and he, Roshell and Meleney went fishing almost every day. The one thing they loved about fishing in the ocean was that you never had a clue as to what you would catch. Sometimes they caught something that was best thrown back in without touching it. Charles felt a great tug on his line and knew he had hooked a big something. He fought the thing for an hour until he finally got it to shore. It was a shark about six foot long. The thing was snapping its teeth together and flopping all over the beach. The two women screamed and dropping their poles and ran up the beach to safety. Charles wanted his leader and hook back so he tried to remove them from the snapping jaws. The thing almost got him a couple of times, so he pulled his father's old Forty-Four out of its holster and dispatched the snapping SOB with a shot between its eyes. The shark laid there and quivered for five minutes, making Charles leery of trying to take his hook from its mouth. The two women came slowly down to the waters edge and looked at the shark. Roshell asked, "What do we do with it hon?"

Charles said, "Some say their mostly good to eat. I had a friend while stationed in France that was an Australian and he said Shark was the fish Aussies cook for Fish and Chips."

Charles had gutted the fifty pound fish out and carried it home and the Aussy had been right., the fish cooked up fine and was delicious to eat.

Charles was restless and didn't have any idea what he was going to do with the rest of his life, that was until he was in town one day and passed the post office and saw a poster that read, "Uncle Sam's Navy, needs you!" He got a funny tingle in his groin and thought he might check this out. He went in and an old grizzled salt in a navy uniform at a desk smiled at him, he had some sort of rank on his right sleeve.

Charles asked, "What does a man have to do to sign up for the navy sir?"

The man asked if he had any prior service and Charles told him two years in France fighting Germans. The old salt asked, "What rank did you hold there."

Charles said, "I was promoted to Captain in the Paris hospital and the French promoted me to Honorary Colonel and made me the commander of an artillery Battalion."

The old navy man came slowly to his feet and stood at attention as he presented a salute to Charles, who without hesitation came to attention and returned it. The old sailor said, "I can't sign you up here Captain, you must go to city hall and they will give you papers to fill out and send to the Department of Navy in Washington DC, but I want to tell you sir, that it is an extreme pleasure to meet you."

He saluted Charles again and after returning the salute Charles left.

He had filled the papers out and forgot all about them. He had been totally shocked to open his door one day a month later and finding an Admiral and his entire entourage standing there. Charles had asked what he could do for them and the Admiral had smiled and said. "Captain, it's hot out here and I was hoping you would ask my men and I into your house"

Charles had reddened to the roots of his hair and apologetically invited them in and made sure they were seated. He introduced his wife and stepmother. The Admiral got right down to business. He said, "My name's Admiral Ricks and I sail a desk for the present in Washington DC. Your application for a commission in the Navy came across my desk and after looking over your records, I grabbed my people and we drove down."

He told Charles, this was a legitimate Navy selection board and it was now convened. Each Naval officer had asked three questions. The questions were mostly about his accomplishments while stationed in France. After each officer had his turn they all looked at the Admiral and nodded their heads. The Admiral had taken his feet then and approached Charles. "You have passed muster young man and are now a Full Lieutenant in the United States Navy. You will attend a navel orientation class in Washington DC and will be assigned to a Destroyer as Executive Officer based here in Norfolk, Virginia. You will spend three months at sea and three months at home. Do you have any questions Lieutenant?"

Charles was in a state of shock and just dumbly shook his head no. The Admiral said, "Good, stand at attention and I will be proud to exchange salutes with our newest Naval officer."

***

The rating came back from break and took the helm. Charles made his notation in the ship's log and went to the galley for some coffee. They were only two days out of Norfolk and he would see his wonderful wife again. There was beginning to be fair communication capabilities in the Navy and ship to shore radios were the coming thing. The skipper had talked to his wife not two days ago and was in the process of fixing it up so everyone aboard could do the same. Everyone who had wives that is.

Charles had his turn the following day. The connection was scratchy, but Roshell's voice still sounded wonderful to him. She said, "I have a wonderful surprise for you when you get home darling."

Charles begged her to tell him now, but she smugly said no, it could wait. After their conversation Charles was in a high state of excitement and didn't really know why. He couldn't even think of what Roshell might have in store for his big surprise. For two days he couldn't concentrate on his job, he just went through the motions automatically.

Charles couldn't believe his eyes, there was his wife and stepmother and his wife had gone and got fat on him. He thought, what a surprise, his wife had put on thirty pounds and was big in the middle. He slowly walked down the gang plank and over to his wife and mother and hugged them both. He put his hands on Roshell's shoulders and held her at arm's length. He shook his head and looked her in the eye and asked if she was eating alright? Roshell realized then he didn't have a clue what her surprise was and said, "You big dummy, this is your surprise, I am five months pregnant with your baby."

Roshell was so tickled that she almost wet her pants. Charles was ecstatic, he was going to be a daddy and it would more than likely happen while he was out to sea. He grabbed his wife and told her she was the most wonderful woman on earth and would make his world come full circle with a child. The son of a gunslinger was a happy man and that's where we leave him for now.

Theodore Potter

OTHER BOOKS PUBLISHED BY:
POTTERHOUSE PUBLISHING

TRUE TALES OF ALASKA AND
THEODORE POTTER'S MEMOIRS

GUNS, GOLD AND TRUE LOVE